PRAISE FOR PETER BENSON'S PREVIOUS NOVELS

THE LEVELS

"A tender and painful first novel... the landscape lends its own magic... I am desperately anxious that this delicate book does not fall on stony ground." – *The Guardian*

"Benson's strong visual sense conjures up vivid imagery from the heart of the countryside." – *The Sunday Times*

"A very apt and unillusioned sort of modern pastoral, blessed with the kind of narrative gift that's like perfect pitch." – *The Guardian*

"A delight – a funny, painful, beautiful book." – Jane Gardam

A LESSER DEPENDENCY

"Peter Benson, through the experiences of this one family, shows how heaven turned into hell... This account of a shocking, shaming business smoulders with quiet anger." – *Time Out*

"A powerful political novel which makes its case all the more forcefully for being so restrained." – *The Guardian*

"This is polemic touched with poetry. Benson's gift is to capture in strong visual terms the earth-based intuition of those 'dropped in the sand and tuned to the rhythms of tiny island life.'" – *The Sunday Times*

"The lack of adornment lends the novel the directness of a folk tale and sharpens its sting." – *The Independent*

"Restrained, deadpan and unaffected, Peter Benson has one of the most distinctive voices in modern British fiction... *The Other Occupant* is a gem of understatement and compassion."
– *The Evening Standard*

"A rare book: compact, exquisitely crafted and intensely upsetting... Benson's cryptic, understated style is ideally suited to the emotive themes which he develops." – *The Sunday Times*

"Layers and crevices, gaps and fissures as important as what is said, all add up to a short novel of power and persuasiveness."
– *Financial Times*

ODO'S HANGING

"The Bayeux Tapestry propels the story of Peter Benson's charming novel. Turold, a master Norman designer of imposing stature and turbulent character, is commissioned by William the Conqueror's half-brother, Bishop Odo, to create the tapestry. Reluctantly, Turold sails for England with his dumb assistant Robert, the story's narrator. The 'real' story evolves side by side with that which the commissioned tapestry records for posterity. And it's a good one."
– *Financial Times*

"The story's narration becomes a dazzling metaphor for the tapestry itself. Robert's musings on the everyday leap into focus with immediacy and poetry... The language overflows with the same imagery of birds, insects, trees, clouds, touchlight and blood as are sewn into the background of the hanging's great tale of conquest." – *Time Out*

"Excellent... A closely observed response to the tapestry – not just an interpretation, but an imaginative act which has its subject's vitality and mystery, its clear gaze at the motives of rulers and the atrocities they cause, and its care for the details of ordinary life."
– *Times Literary Supplement*

"There is a great deal of beautiful writing and thoughtful language here, particularly in the depictions of surfing and sex." – *Time Out*

"Beautifully crafted... by turns touching, funny and erotic, the narrative chronicles the final days of a troubled childhood with a sureness of touch, and the young hero's eventual transformation from son into lover is accompanied by a genuine sense of liberation." – *Times Literary Supplement*

"There is much more to *Riptide* than one of the best sex scenes ever written. It also explores the painful reconciliation between a mother and son who have lived apart for eight years following the death of the boy's father." – *The Daily Mail*

A PRIVATE MOON

"Death itself is the real criminal in this tale, and the real mystery is how we reconcile ourselves to knowing that he will doubtless pull the big job on us one day." – *The Sunday Telegraph*

"Benson's ability to walk this tightrope, between cynicism and sentimentality, between the arbitrariness of death and the absolute value of life, is a measure of his admirable control." – *The Times*

THE SHAPE OF CLOUDS

"Vividly, defiantly realistic at times, luridly surreal at others, his writing's ability to compound striking metaphors of the abstract with a graphic physicality has won him a deserved following." – *Times Literary Supplement*

"Beautiful writing and thoughtful language... page after page of stunning prose." – *Time Out*

"One of the most distinctive voices in modern British fiction." – *Evening Standard*

"A sharp stylist." – *The Sunday Telegraph*

"An adventure story written in Benson s distinctive, flourish-filled style and suffused with his deep and abiding love of the West Country." – *The Daily Mail*

"A coming of age novel that turns the plot of a thriller into a lyrical celebration of the mysterious and enchanting power of the natural world." – *Times Literary Supplement*

"A haunting tale of love, clairvoyance and cannabis." – *The Guardian*

"A *Huckleberry Finn* for the Somerset wilds.' – *The Independent on Sunday*

"*Two Cows and a Vanful of Smoke* mixes Somerset drifters, corrupt police and stolen cannabis, but the real magic – literally – of the book is in its evocation of a mystical English countryside... the prose twists and rolls like a vine creeping over a medieval brick wall." – *New Statesman*

THE SOUTH IN WINTER

Peter Benson

ALMA BOOKS

ALMA BOOKS LTD
3 Castle Yard
Richmond
Surrey TW10 6TF
United Kingdom
www.almabooks.com

First published by Alma Books Limited in 2017
© Peter Benson, 2017

Cover design: nathanburtondesign.com

Peter Benson asserts his moral right to be identified as the author of this
work in accordance with the Copyright, Designs and Patents Act 1988

Printed in Great Britain by CPI Group (UK), Croydon CR0 4YY

ISBN: 978-1-84688-423-8
eBook ISBN: 978-1-84688-424-5

None of the characters in this novel are based on living people and, apart from one incident, none of the events described occurred in Italy in the winter of 2012.

AIRPORT

I went to Italy in February. I had books, a bag of electronics and a suitcase of clothes, and as I sat in the lights of the morning airport, there was cotton in my blood. I'd been awake since half-past three. My feet were cold and my eyes were narrow, and all I wanted to do was stare at the floor. The floor was grey.

I knew where I was, but now, when I think about that time and the box of my body, I had no idea where I was. I didn't know how lost I was, how my thoughts were turning, or how I would find my way back to the place I needed. But this is what early mornings in airports used to do to me. They found a gap in my mind and stripped me. Plastic off wire.

I stared through the windows, watched aeroplanes and waited at a counter for a cup of coffee. I looked at other people. A couple walked by. I didn't know them, but I knew how they were. The woman wanted to be near the window, but the man wanted to sit at the bar. They stopped talking to each other. He picked up a newspaper. She looked at her phone. He sucked his teeth. She shook her head. He pulled a newspaper from his pocket, opened it, sat back, read a page, tutted, turned to the next page, looked at the woman and shook his head. He had a small head and wasn't wearing a tie. She had a small scar on her chin, like a pared nail.

I looked at the cakes and pastries behind the counter, and at the sweets and chocolates by the till. One of the chocolates was long, thin and covered in gold paper, twisted at each end. The woman who was making my coffee was doing that thing coffee-makers do with milk in a steel jug. I dropped my newspaper and, as I picked it up with my left hand, I reached up and slid one of the chocolates into the palm of my hand, transferred it to the folds of my paper and coughed a thief's cough.

My coffee was made. I paid for it, thanked the woman and gave her a smile, carried the mug to a table, sat down and thought about windows. In those days I could write about anything, but had no idea how glass was made, radios worked or eggs were laid, why the sky was blue, the sea was salt or birds sang. I could have found out – I could have educated myself – but I thought there were better things to do with my life.

The coffee was good, and so was the chocolate. In those days, I stole something every couple of weeks, and although I probably had a control disorder or a misalignment of my neuro meta-triggers, in my defence I would say that I understood my impulses and put restraints on them. For example, I never stole anything worth more than a couple of pounds, and I never stole from anywhere that wasn't a chain. So a cheese sandwich from a supermarket, a magazine from a high-street newsagent, a pair of socks from one of those stores that employ Bangladeshi children to make shirts. And yes, I know the arguments. Chains adjust their prices to take account of theft, so if I hadn't stolen that bag of crisps, you'd pay less for your shopping. And my answer? Go and buy yourself a tissue. We all steal and we all rob. We steal from the Bangladeshi child who makes our shirts, and we rob the Costa Rican woman who picked the bananas we slice over our granola. We rob the printer of her health, animals of their lives and the sky of its blue. There's no fine line, no distinction and no peculiarity. Like a colleague who had to leave a demo against a third runway at Heathrow because she wanted to fly to Paris for the weekend, we're all strolling towards the edge so beautifully, all so willing and so attractively dressed, our voices singing "la la la la la la la", our votes cast, our eyes closed and our ears covered with our own dirty hands.

And in my defence I blame nothing or no one. I have no idea why I stole. I didn't get a thrill from doing it. Maybe I could claim that my father or mother or sister led me to warped thoughts and ideas, but I won't. Maybe I was born with them – but maybe I wasn't. Maybe I bred them when I was a child, simply because I didn't have anything better to do. My parents raised me, but didn't know how to raise me. They had values, but their values were worthless. But who knew value could have no worth? Values? Objectivity? Subjectivity? Define value and then ask – who cares?

I stopped thinking about morals and blame and care and values and the end of the world, and I thought about my shoes. Shoes are important. Mine were black and had narrow laces. Then I thought about polish. Where did polish come from? How were brushes made? Why does hot air shimmer? What came first, the orange or the colour? And most crucially, who makes the machines that make the machines? This is how my thoughts used to go. I allowed them to do whatever they wanted, and they did it well. I think they helped me. They made me who I became. My thoughts have taken me to more places than my feet have ever done. I was never cruel or heartless, but I could be forgetful, and I was. I couldn't trust my memory, so I had to keep notes. Sometimes I used the voice memo on my phone, but mostly I used a pen.

I was going to work. In those days, I was envied. People never actually said they wished they had my job, but I know they did. They thought I lived a life of glamour and thrill, for I wrote for the Tread Lightly range of travel guides. My tone varied, but that was the point. I skipped from knowing to nonsense to literary with all stops in between. Sometimes I was purple, sometimes dismissive, sometimes poetic, sometimes chatty. Sometimes I pretended I was leaning on a bar with a drink in my hand, sometimes I spilt the drink, sometimes I laughed, sometimes I said the wrong thing and pretended I didn't understand directions. I could be factual and historical, geographical and epicurean. I used cliché in the literal sense of the word. I pitched my copy as if I was having a conversation with the reader. Less of a guide, more of a friend; less instruction, more ideas; less thought, more insight; less speculation, more truth. Our target market was independent travellers, the ones who are never tourists. They smell of yeast, argue about five euros and panic if they can't find Wi-Fi. They're too cool to chase sights, but that's what they do. The other truth was that sales were falling through the floor. Our target market was migrating to their phones, their blogs and their tablets. These were the facts, though no one talked about them in the office. The office kept their heads down. The office couldn't live with too many facts, and they certainly didn't like the truth.

I'd been briefed to introduce an out-of-season slant to the Italian guide. There was too much stuff about crowds and heat and congestion and nowhere to sit. I bought that. So I was instructed to have a look around, make some notes and write some simple amends. Catch a cold and the February flavour. Change this:

> *If you wish to get away from the crowds and the smell of suntan lotion, dive into the cool and peace of the church of Santa Maria. The heat fades, the sun dims, the windows take the summer and strip it bare, and all you're left with is the sound of the birds in the roof and the gentle scent of frankincense.*

to this:

> *If you want some peace and quiet, the church of Santa Maria is the place to go. Tucked away in a little street behind the main square, its gorgeous interior is an oasis of calm during the high season, a place of peace in the cooler months and, if you're lucky enough to visit in February, a place of the deepest contemplation. For here, as frankincense drifts and the smoke from dying candles twists towards the ceiling, it's easy to imagine yourself in a place where life is always this peaceful, and the simplest things slip into your hands like leaves.*

Some of the work could be done in the office, but the finished guide needed the authenticity of a winter visit, so I'd been given everything south of (and including) Rome, and my colleague, Daniel, had been given the north. My list of places to visit was long enough to allow me to do the job, short enough to cover

in a few weeks. Three? Four? Maybe five? As my editor said as
she flicked a curl of hair out of her eyes, "Just get out there and
do the work". Her name was Cora. The day I met her, I looked
up the meaning of her name. I always look names up, except
when they belong to people I don't want to know anything
about. A person's name, though not chosen by them, accrues
the consequence of everything they do. In Scots, Cora means
"seething pool". In English, it means "maiden". Sometimes, I
thought, differences expose such raging simplicities.

Cora and I started as colleagues. We were colleagues for two
months before we became lovers. We never lived together, but
we did talk about it. It's a boring, normal story. We split, but
we still worked together. We had no choice. She was the editor-
in-chief's editor of choice, I was the editor-in-chief's writer of
choice: times were tough, money was mercury; we couldn't risk
walking away from our jobs. So we moved on. We were mature
adults. I say we were mature adults and moved on, but I suppose we did more than that. I suppose we lived like the keys of
a piano as they wait for the fingers and thumbs.

When Cora walked, people stopped whatever they were doing
to watch her go by, and when she talked, they didn't interrupt.
If she had been a fruit, she would have been an orange. Full and
ripe, and with long, beautiful hair. She always looked like she
was about to explain something to someone stupid, and that
person was usually me. If I had been a fruit, I'd have been a
tomato, and when I told her this, it led to the usual argument
about whether a tomato is a fruit or a vegetable. I won the
argument, though I conceded that you'd never find a tomato in
a fruit salad. "You might," she said, "if you were imaginative

enough." I once told her that sometimes I felt I was the most unimaginative person on the planet, and she didn't disagree. Before I left for Italy, she told me to send her a postcard when I wasn't feeling so sorry for myself, and I said I would. "Make it one with some art on the front," she said.

"I could send you one with a nice view."

"Don't even think about it."

"How about a picture of some nuns eating ice cream?"

"That might work. But I'd prefer a Botticelli."

"OK."

"But don't go out of your way."

"You know I'd go out of my way for you, Cora."

"Yeah. And the Pope's got a balcony. But that doesn't mean he smokes."

"I'm sorry?"

"You will be."

As I sat in the airport drinking coffee and eating stolen chocolate, I knew there was something in the ashes of our relationship. I knew it every time I looked at her, and I thought she knew it when she looked at me, but I had no idea what that something was. Or maybe I did. Maybe I always needed her more than I knew. And maybe she wanted me. The way hearts work baffles me. Contradiction is at the centre of our worlds, and as our worlds orbit, so they leak. But at that time I was travelling too slow to know or understand.

The couple I'd been watching exchanged a couple of words. He looked at his watch. She checked her phone. He looked at her. She looked away. He looked at me. I looked at her. She shook her head at nothing. I thought that maybe this is what would have become of Cora and me. Or maybe we would have resolved our problems and spent our lives gazing into each other's eyes and wondering why we'd ever doubted ourselves. Or maybe we'd have shot each other in a tragic misunderstanding and/or accident outside a pub in Folkestone. Who knows? But we have history, and maybe that's all anyone can hope for. That and owning a few memories, a decent set of saucepans and a toothbrush with medium bristles.

I was basing myself in a place called Atrani on the Amalfi coast. I'd been there before, and was looking forward to seeing it again. You've probably seen pictures of the area. Towns and villages crawl down gorges and valleys into the sea, lemons grow in the hills and little fishing boats bob on the waves. The corniche that runs between Sorrento and Salerno is an advertising chestnut – every week another agency sets up a camera above one of the bends and films a cool couple canoodling in a cabriolet – and every hour a bus driver shakes his fist at a taxi driver. In the season, the Amalfi coast is hot and packed with visitors. I'd checked the weather forecast. It was going to be cold.

I know people who like airports. I don't like airports. I don't like the idea that glamour has been laid on them like sugar on fish. Once, I suppose the glamour was real. Labelled leather suitcases, aluminium aeroplanes with big propellers, men in huge suits, women in hats with scarves around their necks, everyone staring south. The tinkle of ice in glasses, the scent of limes, the smell of luxury. The quiet burble of deference. A string quartet. Now all I heard was disco, and all I smelt was cod.

My phone pinged with a text from Cora. It read: "CEO on a flying visit. Everyone bricking it." I wasn't bricking it. I was cool. It was half-past seven in the morning. I finished my coffee and texted back with "Oh Cora... I wish you were coming with me. You shouldn't be there and I shouldn't be here." I say I texted back, and I did write these words, but my finger hovered over the send button and didn't do what I wanted it to do.

FLYING

I flew to Naples. I sat next to a big man in a blue tracksuit. He was wearing fingerless gloves and eating peanuts. Before he ate, he sucked the salt off each nut before crunching it like a knuckle. He was sweating. I was calm. He was nervous. I was dry. I thought about having a glass of wine.

I read the in-flight magazine, looked at the pictures and thought about perfume. I used to write about perfume for a perfume magazine. Cora wore perfume. When I told her there was perfume and there was perfume, and the perfumes she wore were industrial concoctions that had little to do with the genius of François Rancé or Serge Lutens, she asked me to keep my opinions to myself. I was forty-eight years old, and in those days I didn't notice or remember like I used to. I didn't believe in gods, but I did believe in fate. I saluted magpies and never winked at a pianist. I flayed, thrashed my arms at the world and, when I had to, I told my sorrows to the stones. I was, I think, in my wilderness years. Those years that creep up on you in a dark alley and don't even bother to mug you; they revel in the cold, slip a bad penny in your pocket and wait for you to find it. And once you've found it and allowed it to infect you, all you can do is let it do its work. One day, you think, these years will leave me. They're nothing to worry about, for they might not even be years. They might just be a few months, and the coin they carry might be a stone.

The woman with the trolley offered me a drink. She had a weary, closed look, and the eyes of someone for whom time is hands on a clock. Not enough sleep, not enough peace, too many drunks, too many flights and too many trains. We recognized something in each other, or I thought we did. Too many flights between us, too many places half-seen and barely remembered. Life was just another job for both of us. I said: "Can I have a coffee, please?"

"Of course, sir."

"Milk and sugar?"

"Milk, no sugar."

She made the drink, put a paper napkin on my table and set the plastic cup in front of me. I gave her money, thanked her, raised the drink to my lips and sipped. It was hot and poor, and as it slipped down I felt it drag my thoughts with it. I was a lucky man. I didn't deny it. I was being paid to do what millions of people would kill to do. I raised the cup again and became aware that the peanut man was looking at me. I turned to look at him and raised the cup another inch, and said, "Cheers." He looked through me. His eyes were dull. He didn't acknowledge my greeting. He held my gaze until I had to look away, and then he took another peanut out of the packet and sucked its salt away.

Maybe the idea of wilderness years was a nonsense and I'd simply seen too much, done too much and visited too many places. I'd stayed in too many hotels, opened too many empty cupboards and slept in too many beds. Sometimes people have mistaken me for what my mother would call a "gentleman of the road", a solitary who wanders from town to town, maybe the lonely Ahasver or maybe not, maybe just someone looking for something he lost but not remembering what that thing is. Other people have said I could be a professional musician who forgot how to play his instrument, or a thief who always returns his pickings. But I wasn't beyond redemption. I always said "Please" and "Thank you", and I always chose the smallest biscuit. I was the dog in the street that saw a sausage, but checked it wasn't someone else's before picking it up, and I was the cat on the warm bonnet, the rabbit at its hole with twitchy whiskers. I suppose there's truth in all these things, but don't mistake this honesty for anything else. In those days I had goals. I didn't just write stuff for Tread Lightly. I'd written two novels. I'd written a screenplay based on a novel written by a famous writer I met once in a bar. I'd written the pilot for a radio sitcom and I had a great idea for a kids' book. I was full of ideas. I hadn't been published or broadcast, but I did have an agent. He'd tried to sell both my novels but hadn't had any luck; the publishers' lists were always full or they weren't looking for a book set in an existential dystopia narrated by a deaf child. They usually wished me luck and all the best, and one editor even said she'd enjoyed the first one and would be interested in reading the second. But when I finished it – a travel book set on the Caledonian Road, London N1, in which the traveller doesn't travel more than two miles but manages to see the whole of the world by visiting a wide range of shops, salons, offices and homes – she'd left the publisher to get married and raise rare-breed chickens in Cornwall. It's a cruel world. But all is not lost. I believe that once is a long time and can be more than twice.

TAXI

I was met at Naples airport by a driver with dark sunglasses, a padded jacket and a hand-written sign that misspelt my name – MATTHEW BASTAR. He offered to carry my bags, but I told him I could manage. I followed him to the car park, sat in the back of his taxi, and he drove away. He asked me what I was doing in his country, and I explained. I speak good Italian, Spanish and Portuguese. I have some German and a few words of Russian. An aptitude for languages is probably the only real talent I have, although I used to be able to do a couple of card tricks. The driver nodded and said he liked tourists. Winter was a bad time for him, so he was grateful for a big fare. He told me to relax and enjoy the trip.

The outskirts of Naples are the outskirts of any city. Narrow your eyes, block out the street ads and Vesuvius, and you could be driving through the outskirts of Salamanca, Manchester, Athens, Melbourne, Winnipeg or Casablanca. Take your pick. The traffic chokes, the kids on scooters swerve, men cross the road without looking, women hang from their balconies and shout, children play in parks. Washing flaps, policemen yawn, clouds churn. I texted Cora to tell her I'd landed, settled back and closed my eyes for half an hour.

I like to snooze. It's one of my greatest pleasures. I like the half-dreams, the knowledge that I'm almost conscious, the inevitability of the images, the gentle relief when I wake and the taste of sleep in my mouth – the feeling that I'm truly alive, doing what I was put on this world to do, living the life Ryōkan believed in. And so it was. And I half-dreamt of Cora. We were in bed and she was laughing at something I'd said. At one point she got out of bed and walked across the room to the window, and as she did I watched the curve of her back as it caught the light. I could see the dusting of tiny hairs that grew along the line of her spine, and hear her naked feet as they brushed the carpet. When she turned around, she was holding a hedgehog in one hand and a rabbit in the other. The two animals looked at each other and then looked at me. I could smell them in the dream, and they smelt of cheese. I woke as the driver took a bend on the climb into the mountains beyond the city, and as he took another, the first of the netted lemon orchards appeared by the road, the sea shone and Capri appeared in a distant haze.

I'd written about Capri for the guide. The place is the antithesis of everything Tread Lightly stands for – exclusive shops, crowds, the desire to be seen, expensive souvenirs – but I'd liked the place. It was honest and beautiful and bold, and when the crowds went home in the evening it was easy to imagine you had the island to yourself, and easier to understand why the rich and celebrated loved the place. But my copy hadn't pleased Cora. She'd wanted less stress on the ghosts of the famous who haunted the villas and bars, and more on the fact that a paradise had been ruined by overexposure. When I pointed out that we were as guilty of overexposing the place as Oscar Wilde, Rita Hayworth and Maria Callas ever were, she tried to remind me that we were committed to "treading lightly". I reminded her that "Tread Lightly" was a brand dreamt up by a copywriter as he flew to New York on Concorde. And we were having a good day.

When we reached the Amalfi coast and the corniche, I wound the window down and stared at the cliffs, the gorges, the villas, the bridges, the arches, the restaurants and the sky. The world felt good and beautiful, and I could believe the brief made more than sense. I could believe C.S. Lewis was right when he said "We don't have souls. We are souls..." – and as we cruised through the tunnels and dropped into Amalfi, it made perfect sense. I came up with a saying of my own. I turned it over in my mind and then I wrote it in my notebook: "*We don't have credit cards. We are the credit.*"

ATRANI

In Atrani I had an apartment with a view of the village and the coast, the lights of Maiori and the ships heading for Salerno. The floors were marble and oil paintings hung on the walls. A glass cabinet contained a collection of porcelain animals with huge eyes. The woman who owned the place showed me how to work the heater and explained that sometimes it was difficult to open the door onto the terrace. Her name was Arabella. She had a wide mouth, dark eyes and wore her clothes like a beast wears its smile. I couldn't take my eyes off the collar of her coat. It was sharp and red and sparkled. She wrote her number on a card and told me to ring if I needed anything. I told her I had everything I needed and reached out to shake her hand. Her hand felt like cake. She held on for longer than I expected, then let go, wrapped a scarf around her face and left me alone.

I spent an hour doing the things I used to do when I landed on a job. I moved a table to take advantage of the view, set up my laptop, stacked my books in a pile, put my washbag in the bathroom and folded my clothes into drawers. I see myself in the order I create, and my creation is a type of order. And when I'd done everything that needed doing, I made a cup of coffee, sat down, opened my notebook and wrote something about the view. It was beautiful, idyllic, everything an Italian view could be. The tower of the church rose over a whitewashed tumble of houses, shirts flapped on lines, shuttered windows creaked, the road wound below the houses and the sea lapped onto a crescent of sand. In the distance the coastline rose and fell past Salerno towards Paestum and, overhead, the sun hung in a pale-blue sky. I heard bells and someone singing, and the smell of my coffee was sweet. When I'd finished it, I closed my book and walked into Atrani.

The apartment was on a narrow alley of steps and turns and twists and tunnels and dives, more hanging washing, people snoring, dogs growling, Madonnas watching. It was early afternoon, and I had the place to myself. In season, the place filled with people, some clutching copies of the *Tread Lightly Guide*, chasing my words about the Piazza Umberto, hoping for a bed at the A' Scalinatella and updating their Facebook status at the Birecto café. Now the shops were shuttered, the bars dark, the hostel closed. A cat was snoozing in a doorway, and as I strolled through the arches and onto the beach, even the gulls ignored me. I sat on a bench, pulled out my notebook and wrote:

The Amalfi Coast comes into its own during the winter, when the locals can claim back – albeit for the shortest time – their pretty towns and villages. The hordes have gone, the madness is over, the only sound comes from the sea as it washes the empty beaches and slaps against the hulls of the colourful boats. For the traveller who really wants to experience the place at its best, February is the

time to visit. Forget the cold and rain (for this is always a
possibility) and give yourself the gift of endless surprise.
Every corner, every forgotten alley, every deserted path offers
a promise, and...

I stopped writing. I looked at the sea. I looked at my words.
I wondered. I thought about Cora and her beautiful laugh. I
looked at the sea again, turned around and left the beach to
itself.

RAIN

I left the beach to itself, wandered into the town square, found a bar, drank a beer, ate some pasta, watched some television football and listened to men argue about fishing. I scribbled some ideas for my kids' book. It was going to be set in Paris and feature a little boy, a kindly gentleman and the market where caged birds are sold. I wrote a first sentence, crossed it out, wrote a second first sentence, thought about it, crossed that one out, drank an espresso, paid the bill, and then climbed the steps to my apartment. I opened the door. I stepped inside. I closed the door. I turned on the light. I walked down the corridor to the sitting room. I stood by the table. I looked at the floor. Sometimes life is easiest when all you do is one simple thing after another. Sometimes the last thing you want to do is complicate life by thinking about what might have been. Sometimes you have to resist the temptation to phone someone you love.

The apartment was cold. The single heater was useless. I poured a glass of wine and sat to watch the lights of the town, the coast road and the ships at sea. It started to rain. It rained for ten minutes and then it began to sleet. The wind blew, the shutters rattled, the waves crashed below my window. I thought about phoning the woman who owned the place and telling her I wanted my money back and was moving into a hotel in Amalfi, but I didn't. I went to the bedroom, piled six blankets onto the bed, climbed in, tucked my hand under the pillow and tried to sleep.

I was in that place where you're drifting and the edge of the first dream is peeping around the corner when my phone pinged. I was going to ignore it, but I couldn't. I knew it was Cora. I reached out, grabbed it, pulled it under the bedclothes and read the text: "Hey. Brian been and gone. Restructuring at the office. You're safe but Chris fired! Speak tomorrow. Hope you're warm."

Brian was the CEO. Chris was the editor-in-chief and an ally, but now he had gone, and the chances were that Cora had been promoted. I think that was what the exclamation mark meant. The thought was interesting. With his power in her hands, my security wasn't a given. But maybe it was. I was confused. I thought about texting back, but I didn't. I didn't, because I don't like texting. I know people who claim it's a new poetry, a new paradigm, a new this, a new that. I think it's an excuse. I use it, but only because I have to. And before you tell me that I don't have to do anything, consider the lilies of the field. Or consider something else. Just don't tell me what I don't have to do. I pulled on my trousers and went for another glass of wine.

Cora once told me that my drinking was out of control. "If you don't quit, I will," she said. I suppose that was the gist and end of it, and although I could get incapable, I'd developed the ability to create capability from my incapability. An impossible, I know, but I do have some talents. And I also know how to cook scrambled eggs.

RAVELLO

Before redemption comes realization, and before realization comes Ravello. And after Ravello comes nothing but a slow glide to the pebbled shore and our hastening minutes, and the cruel hand.

A lot of words have been wasted about Ravello, about how it perches on a cliff, about the views from the terraces and gardens, and about how Wagner, Huston, Lawrence, Garbo, Sting and other great artists have been drawn to the place. I took the bus in the morning, through the last kick of rain and sleet, along the corniche and into the clouds. I drank coffee in a café on the piazza, allowed the pleasures to swim in my blood, and then wandered off to visit the Villa Cimbrone.

If Ravello is the place to go and escape the few people who stroll the streets in off-season Amalfi, then the garden of the Villa Cimbrone is the place to visit if you want complete isolation. The Villa itself, now converted into one of the smartest hotels on the coast (is it? Check...) will be closed, and the chance to visit Gore Vidal's former home, the fabulous La Rondinaia, denied by ropes and signs, but the rest of the garden will be yours. And what a garden it is. A gorgeous formal walk leads to the famous terrace of infinity, surely one of the most photographed spots in the whole of the country.

The immense views, the precipitous drop, the busts' blank eyes, the perfect blend of artifice with the natural world – it would take a cynical mind not to be awed by the place, the silence and the feeling that this is a place apart, a God's sneeze from heaven...

Maybe Cora's text had put me right, but once again I was feeling OK about writing this stuff. It was a job. Someone had to do it. I knew people who wrote job descriptions for a living, copy designed to recruit bankers, accountants, technical-support officers and oil-well operators. At least I could pretend to be creative, rather than just aim for it. And if people wanted to visit Italy in February, then they should have some idea of what to expect.

Famous for its music festival, Ravello should also be fêted for its spectral winter atmosphere, when the perfect little streets shine with rain and echo to nothing but one set of footsteps – yours. A perfect surprise awaits you at every corner. Here a startled cat drops into a hidden lemon orchard, there a glimpse into a deserted courtyard that could have delighted and inspired Wagner (was he inspired or did he just hang out? Check: can't afford to irritate any Wagnerians...). And if you take a stroll through the Villa Rufolo, further delights await.

It was lunchtime, and the weather hadn't improved. I returned to the piazza, ordered a beer and something hot, and sat to watch the locals shout at each other. Cora and I used to shout at each other, but never in the Italian way, never about a simple thing like, say, the colour of a pair of trousers. Cora and I used to shout about serious things. Drinking, sex, work, if we were ever going to live together, cakes, France, gardening, colours, the shape of clouds. OK, so I'm contradicting myself, but I'm allowed a few luxuries. And now, listening to the people of Ravello as they argued about the best way to cook sardines, I was struck by the thought that maybe Cora and I were more suited than we thought. There were enough opposites going on – she liked salami, didn't like gloomy Scandinavian composers and always kept a vase of flowers on her desk – but there was enough to think that we might have had a future. When we were good, we were better than anyone I'd been with, and she'd said the same. We could be comfortable together for an hour without saying a word to each other; we both disliked shopping; we both enjoyed German cinema; we both enjoyed spending weekends at the coast. She liked tomatoes and I liked tomatoes. These things were more than most people had. And at that moment, as I thought about Wim Wenders and his crazy hair, she phoned.

BUSY

"Hi."

"Hi."

"How's it going?"

"Not bad. The apartment's freezing and it's been raining for the last twenty-four hours, but I've got some stuff done."

"Good for you."

"Why do these places have marble floors?"

"What places?"

"Mediterranean apartments."

"I don't know. Tell me. Is this meant to be a joke? Why do Mediterranean apartments have marble floors?"

"I've no idea. Maybe they're cool in the summer."

"There you go."

"But on a winter morning in bare feet – you've no idea."

"I think I have," she said, and she laughed. It was just a small one, but it was a laugh.

"So, what happened with Chris?"

She coughed, but it wasn't a sinister cough. It didn't mean anything. "Brian told him straight. You know what he's like. Said he'd been coasting for too long and they needed someone who understands digital. Someone with balls. Gave him half an hour to clear his desk, and then they escorted him from the building."

"Shit."

"Exactly."

"And they gave his job to someone with balls?"

"Oh yes."

"And who was that, Cora?"

"Guess."

"Do I have to?"

"You do."

I laughed. "Congratulations."

"Thank you."

"You…" I hesitated here. "You deserve it."

"You sound like you almost mean it."

"I do. The best woman won."

"Things are going to change around here…"

"And what does that mean?"

"You'll see. But don't worry. Finish what you're doing. I'm not cancelling any live projects. And I'm open to suggestions about new ones. That one you had about cargo-ship voyages. I still like the sound of it. We could turn it into a new series."

"Cool."

"And any other ideas you might have. Let me know."

"OK."

"You know, Matt…"

"What?"

"Whatever's happened between us, or whatever might happen – we're professionals, right?"

"Right."

"And even though you've never remembered my birthday, you're still the best writer in the building."

"Cheers."

"But that's the only compliment you're getting. So go back to work, and don't call me unless it's urgent. I'm busy."

"Cora?"

"Yes?"

I thought about saying something, something about regretting not remembering her birthday and wishing I'd told her – at least once – that she smelt of pears and lemons and all the fruits I loved the most, but I stopped myself. If she was a busy woman, then I was a busy man, and we were past the grief of things not said. "I'll be in Naples tomorrow, then Rome."

"I know. I've got your itinerary in front of me. Anything else?"

"Not really."

"OK," she said, and then she was gone and I put my phone in my pocket while the Italians in Ravello argued on about sardines.

NAPLES

I love Naples. Some people will say that this is a lie, for Matt Baxter is incapable of love. He can like and he can hate, and he might even be able to lust, but he's like every writer. His love is an illusion, and although he thinks he knows stuff, his knowledge leaks. He's lost in his own thoughts, and everything he doubles is tripled by his debt. He could spend a lifetime standing at a crossroads and still not understand the meaning of direction. This doesn't explain anything, but do I care? No I don't. Which is why people say these things. But I digress.

I love Naples. I love the place because – at the risk of trotting out a cliché – she is the perfect woman. Dirty, sophisticated, hidden, exposed, dangerous, beautiful, lost, undiscovered, trodden, dark, noisy, white, sick, slick, wicked, loving, painted, full. Give me an adjective and I'll give you Naples. Give me a couple of days and Naples will show you nothing. Or everything. And then write some lines.

The terror of Naples is its beauty and its charm. Threat appears to lurk on every corner (not every corner, surely, revise this), but approach the threat and it will smile a welcome. And everywhere you go, the smell of blood and religion crackles like fire.

Unlike many of the great cities of Italy, Naples never feels cramped by tourists. Maybe its reputation precedes it, but that's to the traveller's advantage, for here you can wander the streets without bumping into the packs of sightseers that infest Rome, Florence, Pisa and Venice. And if you choose to visit in February, your pleasure can be doubled, for at this time of year you can visit the Chiesa del Pio Monte della Misericordia and stand alone for half an hour in front of Caravaggio's Seven Acts of Mercy *with only the dust motes for company...*

OK, so my prose flies from black to purple in a twitch, but I'm old enough to know what I can do. And so did Caravaggio. And I also believe the reason Western art in the twenty-first century is the epitome of mediocrity is because Western artists in the twenty-first century fail to understand who their true patrons are. But don't let me digress. Don't let me compare the Medici with HSBC. Don't let me tell you that the last great British writer died in 1966, the last American one in 2012, or the last German one in 1962. I know nothing about Japanese novelists or Canadian playwrights or Sudanese poets, but I'll bang on until the sea comes to the river.

Caravaggio's *Seven Acts of Mercy* is sublime, and when you stand in front of it, you understand why the paintings in the other churches you might wander into are hidden in unlit side chapels. The man didn't bow to his subject, his patron or his guilt; he took everything, spilt their drinks, threatened them with fire and wrung them dry. He made a new world from the old, one where the present was truth, the past was a mine and only the subject lied.

In one corner of the painting, a rich man offers a beggar his coat. In another, a woman offers her starving father the milk from her breast. The woman's face shines with light, and the look in her eyes reminded me of someone. Caravaggio would have liked the person I was thinking about, although I know he was in constant trouble and would not have stayed long enough to ask her for a glass. But who does stay long enough? The saint or the fool? And how, I wondered, can some people create masterpieces when they are in such pain or alarm or dread? Caravaggio under a sentence of death, Plath wailing in Fitzroy Road, Beethoven weeping with tinnitus, Kahlo burning with gangrene, Handel screaming as the surgeon cut into his eyeball, Manolete speeding towards Linares, Billie Holiday looking for a vein, Picasso staring into the moon, while the rest of us do nothing but complain. But what do I know?

THE SECRET ROOM

The daughter in the *Seven Acts of Mercy* reminded me of Cora, but in the Secret Room of the Museo Archeologico Nazionale I found her portrait. I say portrait, but it wasn't a portrait of her face. As a grateful Roman gentleman of leisure reclines upon a couch, a woman with a fabulous bottom kisses his neck, squats and lowers herself on him.

The painting is one of a collection recovered from Pompeii's brothels. Some archaeologists believe they represent a pictorial menu of what was on offer, though others think they were simply pre-coital stimulants. Whatever, the Secret Room contains not only a great range of paintings, but also garden ornaments in the shape of enormous phalli. Bronze dildos hang in profusion, and a marble of Pan giving a handsome length to a surprised goat completes the entertainment. After this, the other exhibits in the museum – Roman heads, vanilla frescoes from Pompeii and Herculaneum, some mosaics, a collection of vases your mother might like – pale. Downstairs, I stood in front of a sculpture of a pair of muscular brothers tying a woman to a bull, and stopped to look at some little sculptures in glass cases, but was drawn back to the Secret Room.

I was standing in front of the paintings from Pompeii again when I heard the sound of voices. A group of French schoolchildren was heading towards the room, their squeals of anticipation echoing in the vast halls. I had moved on and was once again inspecting the rutting Pan. The squeals grew louder and closer, higher and higher, when suddenly, from behind a wall, a Neapolitan woman of gravity, size and power appeared and stood by the entrance. She held up her hand, said "No…" and pointed to a sign that stated children under a certain age were not permitted to enter. An accompanying teacher attempted to rally morale, but it was to no avail. Never has Gallic arrogance taken such a fall, and as the children were led away to study a collection of coins, I turned back to take another look at Cora in the ancient world.

DRINK

Italians drink, on average, three cups of coffee a day, or maybe it is six. The agreed number will be somewhere in a Tread Lightly Guide, as will a remark about how tourists insist on ordering cappuccinos when to get a true taste of Italian café culture an espresso, enjoyed standing at the bar, is the only way to go.

I found a café and ordered an espresso, enjoyed it standing at the bar, ordered another and, as the caffeine hit, perused a line of bottles. It wasn't time for an aperitivo, but I felt the need, and the need was strong.

The usual exotics were lined up on the shelves, the ones with pretty labels and names you remember from a party in Deptford with nurses, and for a moment I thought about ordering a glass of Cynar. Cynar is sherry made from artichokes, but who would drink stuff like that when a bottle of Jack Daniels was winking from its perch? I said, "Jack Daniels?" The barman raised his eyebrows and looked at his watch. I pulled 10 euros from my pocket, put it on the bar and watched it uncurl. He shrugged, took down the bottle, poured a good shot and folded his arms to watch.

I drank. I held the first gulp in my mouth, felt it solder the insides of my cheeks, waited, swallowed and listened. I heard music, lutes and accordions and drums beating. A poet appeared in my head and whispered a line about flowers. For is there anything better than the first swallow of the day? There isn't. The second? Maybe. I swallowed the second, and as it met the caffeine it created a little explosion in my head. I felt the pop, ignored the feeling and went for some more. Maybe I was wanting, maybe I was rash. Whatever. The feeling put me in mind of the office, my flat, the pub on the corner of my street, buskers, adverts on the tube, the Jubilee Line, London Bridge station, rain, Christmas crackers, one perfect Christmas in the 1980s, Shakespeare, the smell of aviation fuel, bananas, the gas they use to ripen bananas – and Cora. Another swallow and all the other thoughts failed, dived off a cliff of my own devising, and Cora remained. She stood in front of me, slipped out of a blue dress, turned, bent her back, smiled and told me to write 2,000 words about the Dordogne by lunchtime. She could be like that. She could be perfect.

SNOOZE

Cora could be perfect. Did I think that about anyone else? No I didn't, and I never had. I ordered another Jack. It was as good as the first. It didn't bite my stomach and remind me that in an hour's time it would be trying to nip its way out of my stomach. It was smooth and glossy, and sweet.

Cora's lips were sweet. They tasted sweet, looked sweet and puckered like sweets. Her breath smelt of chocolate – and sometimes, when she was tired and drifting towards sleep, she used to put her lips together and make little popping sounds. I leant towards the barman and opened my mouth to say something about her. "Another?" he said, and I said, "Cora."

There was nothing to do after the second Jack but retire to my hotel and lie down. I was staying in a room with a view over the Piazza Bellini. I took my time getting back to my room, but once I'd found it I lay down, stared at the ceiling for however long it took, then snoozed for a couple of hours. When I awoke, the air was full of the sound of firecrackers. I got out of bed, walked to the window, opened the curtains and looked down. Students were having a party in the square, dancing or talking in little knots of fun.

I'd been having an end-of-the-world dream, one of my recurrers. The details change, but the theme remains the same. I'm on the run from a calamitous event that signals the end of civilization, and everywhere people are in panic. They're wailing, fighting, running, desperate, uncomprehending, lost – and I know I'm going to be caught and bound before being killed and eaten by a large man wearing trousers made from dog skins. Someone once tried to interpret it for me, but she just wanted dominion over me. I told her that her idea of the end-of-the-world representing sexual repression was nonsense, and the notion that running represented impotence was even more ridiculous. But what can you do? I turned away from the window and the happy students, padded to the bathroom, stood in the shower for ten minutes and then wrapped myself in towels.

Towels are – like snoozing – another of my pleasures. I used every one I could find, lay back down and checked my phone. Cora had left two texts and one voice message.

Text 1: "You there?"

Text 2: "Hello Matt? Call when you've got a minute."

Voice message: "Matt? It's me. Nothing important. Just wanted to check progress. I had a call from Daniel in Genoa. Sounds like he's got some real weather up there." There was the sound of rustling paper and distant phones. "OK, call when you've got a minute."

SAYING NOTHING

"Hi."

"Hi."

"How's Naples?"

"I love her. I want her taste on me all day and all through the night."

"What?"

"You heard me. I was walking down this street, and thought about you."

"What does that mean?"

"It means I thought about you."

"Yes. I know. But in the context of Naples being your lover…"

"I didn't mean it like that. But now you come to think of it…"

"God…"

"What?"

"If you think I'm ready to get into a bit of phone sex, think again."

"Oh go on, Cora. You know you want to."

"I'd rather die."

"I don't think you would. Not really. If someone said to you, look, Cora, here's the choice: either you have phone sex with Matt – who is, by the way, lying wrapped in a six damp towels on his hotel bed – or you take a bullet to the brain. I think I know what you'd choose."

"Now you're making me nauseous."

"I'm glad we can still have a laugh."

"Is that what you call it? I call it a sad attempt to make me smile."

"I know you are."

"What?"

"Smiling. I can tell."

"How?"

"By the tone of your voice."

"You need to remember who you're talking to. I'm more than just your editor..."

"Sure. But then I'm more than just a hack."

"Everyone else thinks you're exactly that. OK, you might be a good one, but don't let it go to your head."

"I started to write my kids' book."

"What kids' book?"

"The one I've started to write."

She sighed.

"But then I crossed out what I'd written."

"Why?"

"Because I'm a perfectionist."

She took a deep breath. I heard it, hot against the receiver, its air filled with the desire she felt a need to deny. She was hot and beautiful, and her lips tasted of oranges. "So," she said, "Naples..."

"It's fine, Cora. Cold, but fine. I've seen a Caravaggio, drunk some coffee, done the street-food thing and watched some students trying to set fire to themselves. I'll have some good copy. I've got a couple more things to see, then I'll be in Rome."

"Fine."

"And the office?"

"I think you'll like the changes…"

"Oh, tell me all."

"You'll have to see them for yourself. Show, not tell. That's how we live, isn't it?"

"So I'm told."

"Then you'll have to wait and see."

"Cora?"

"Yes?"

I thought about being bold, but then I thought about being sensible. "Nothing."

"Good. Keep in touch," she said, and then she hung up.

PIZZA

I know. It's an old saw, but Naples is the only place for pizza. A thin base topped with tomato, garlic, basil and anchovies. A jug of new wine, the sound of a heartbroken singer on a crackling radio. The sleepy stare of a Neapolitan waiter, the shouting from rooms upstairs, the crying of a wronged woman in the street, a grey cat with white paws. What more could I want? Because although I was comfortable with my own company and could sit on my own and enjoy the bustle and the solitude, sometimes I missed looking across a table into the eyes of someone I cared for. Sometimes I missed talking about what we were going to do next. Sometimes I missed sharing a fork of food. Sometimes I missed the smell of someone else's toothpaste on the pillow, and sometimes I missed hearing a mumbled dream word in the middle of the night. Sometimes I missed sitting on a bed to wait for someone to finish in the bathroom, and sometimes I missed the familiarity of a shaking head.

I found a restaurant that won't be featuring in the latest edition of the *Tread Lightly Guide* to Italy. Why? Because although I might encourage people to visit some places, I keep the perfect places to myself. I will say that it was on a street in the *centro storico*, the waiter was grumpy, the cook was very old and the anchovies were flipping as he dropped them on the tomato. The posters on the wall were torn, and the tablecloth was checked and sticky. What more could you want? I knew exactly what more I wanted.

I quartered the pizza. I forked it. I cut it. I ate it. I wiped my chin. I cut some more. I poured some wine. I drank the wine. It tasted of almonds and burnt sawdust. I looked at the waiter. He yawned at me. I sliced some more. The radio snapped off, the television flickered. Football. I watched the gods as they passed the ball: the gods played in the rain – the pizza got better with every bite. The wine took on different flavours – here was lemon and there was cinnamon – and as I wiped my plate with a hunk of bread, Napoli scored. The waiter clapped his hands, did a small dance, and for a moment I thought he was going to have a heart attack. The cook came from the kitchen to watch the replay and returned to his work with a hand-shaped imprint of flour on his forehead.

The waiter took my plate. "Good?"

"The best," I said, and ordered an espresso.

I stayed until half-time, drank my coffee slowly, paid my bill and launched myself at the night. I was going to head back to my hotel, but I stopped at a bar, parked myself at a corner table, ordered a brandy, took out my notebook and wrote a few lines:

Guinness doesn't travel further west than Dublin, Cornish pasties won't cross the Tamar and pizza can't travel farther than Naples without feeling homesick. What do these cooks (do they call them cooks? check) do that no one else can do? After all, what could be more simple than a thin crust of dough, a spread of tomato, some chunks of mozzarella, a hint of garlic and basil, a couple of anchovies, all cooked in a wood-fired oven? But what could be more difficult to get right? And what could be more welcoming on a freezing Neapolitan night, with sleet lashing the misted windows of a little place in the centro storico?

I could think of a lot of things. I finished my drink, headed into the sleet and sailed back to my hotel. I kicked my shoes off, stood at the window and watched the piazza. Some students were arguing about something. Dante? Spaghetti? Violins? Weed? I had no idea. I turned, sat on the bed, took my phone from my bag and stared at the blank screen. It was half-past ten. I opened my notebook. I was going to write a poem.

My pen hovered. I don't believe in rules – not for writing or anything else – but I do believe a poem should be hard-won, pulled screaming and fighting out of the writer's head.

My poem wasn't going to be about a house, a random feeling, a plate of rice or a wheelbarrow. It wasn't going to be one of those simple things that drops from a pen like a bird drops off a fence to catch the drowsy worm. This was going to be right, and its words were going to absorb the feelings behind them, hold them tight and never let go. They were going to pinch. I wrote a couple of lines, read them out loud, crossed them out, wrote them again, wondered if I had the gift, wondered if there was such a thing as a gift and then closed my notebook. I closed my notebook, laid back and closed my eyes, and was gone.

FIRED

I dreamt that Spandau Ballet, the New Romantic pop group, were running a sports shop in Halifax. They had a special offer on cricket bats for left-handed cricketers, and I called in to buy one for my friend, David Gower, the most elegant and preternaturally gifted batsman of his generation. The problem was that all the bats had red handles, and I knew that David didn't like red. He liked blue. I explained this to Tony Hadley (Spandau Ballet's vocalist), who went to talk to Martin Kemp (one-time bassist, but now cricket-bat adapter). While he did this, I woke up. It was half-past one in the morning – half-past twelve in London. My mouth was wired and dry. I opened a bottle of water, took a long drink and then sat up in the bed and surfed the television. I found a programme about the euro currency crisis. Things were not looking good. A man in a blue suit said something about countries and dominoes, and a woman wearing black boots asked another man if Greece was too big to fail. I thought about size and failure and Spandau Ballet for a couple of minutes, came to no conclusions, stood up, lay down again and checked my phone. I had no messages. I stared at the screen for a moment and then I called Cora.

The phone rang for half a minute, and then she picked up. She was not happy. She'd been asleep.

"Matt! What's going on? Do you know what time it is?"

"No."

"It's almost one o'clock."

"I started to write a poem for you."

"What the…"

"It's a poemy poem."

"You're drunk."

"No I'm not."

"Yes you are. I know you."

"I had some wine earlier, but that doesn't mean I'm so drunk."

"You had half a dozen, and you're only halfway there."

"Cora…"

"Oh please, Matt. What do you want?"

"I just," I said, "I just wanted to say that I started to write you a poem. And I saw you today."

"How could you see me today? I'm in London. You're in Naples."

"In the Archaeological Museum. You were in a Roman fresco."

"Was I?"

"Yes."

"And what was I doing in a Roman fresco?"

"Saying hello to a very grateful man."

There was a sigh, and I heard the rustle of bedclothes. I remembered the smell of her bedclothes – the smell of lavender and basil. She lived in East Dulwich, in a top-floor flat with a view of gardens and other houses from her bedroom window. Sometimes we spent all Sunday in the bed she was lying in now. I knew those sheets. They were pale green. Or pale blue. With matching pillowcases. She liked two pillows and I liked one. Sometimes we'd spend all Sunday talking about nothing in particular and trying not to think about Monday. Sometimes I'd cook her scrambled eggs.

"So you've called me in the middle of the night to tell me that you think you saw me in some old painting."

"It wasn't an old painting. It was a fresco. From Pompeii."

"And a fresco isn't a painting?"

"Well, I suppose it is. Technically. But…"

"And what made you think it was me?"

"She had your body. Your arse."

Silence again.

"OK, Matt. Here's the thing. I want to sleep. You've got to work in the morning. I've got to work in the morning…"

"But Cora…"

"And if I feel like it, I could fire you now."

I laughed.

"In fact I think I will."

"Please, Cora…"

"You're fired."

"What?"

"You heard."

"But you can't. You can't fire me…"

"I just did."

I let a silence come down the line. Then I said: "Do you remember that day a pink flower appeared on your cactus? It was a Sunday…"

"Matt. I have no idea what you're talking about."

"Cora. Please."

"Please nothing." She took a long, tired breath. "I want you on the first plane in the morning. You can come into the office, clear your desk and forget about coming back."

"Cora!"

"No," she said, and the phone went dead.

I lay on the bed and stared at my feet. I looked at my phone. I tossed it away. I picked it up and pressed redial. It rang for half a minute, then went to voicemail.

I picked up the notebook and opened it to the poem I'd started. It had an empty heart, but I wrote a few more lines, and by the time I was ready to go back to sleep I had enough nonsense to stun a horse. The horse looked at me and dared me to do it. I ripped the page from the book, screwed it into a ball, tossed it across the room and turned my face to the wall.

HALF A SAINT'S LEG

I was raised a Protestant, flirted for six months with Buddhism, had a brief fling with Taoism and, although I moved in with atheism, I still wonder about Christianity. I wonder if I'll burn in the eternal fires of hell, but when I'm faced with the iconography of Catholicism, I know I'm OK. I'm not talking Caravaggio here, or Piero della Francesca, or Palestrina, or any of the other geniuses who took a shilling from their patrons – what I'm talking about is the idea that the congealed blood of San Gennaro (martyred over 1,700 years ago) liquefies on cue three times a year – the irony being that if it doesn't, Naples will have bad luck. And I'm also talking about the even wilder sight I found in the museum of the Angevin church of Santa Chiara.

The peaceful cloisters of the church are famous for their majolica tiles, and are a perfect – if riotous – balm after a heavy night of being fired. The museum contained pieces of the church salvaged from the remains of allied bombing in World War II, the busts of dead bishops and, at the back, the excavated remains of a Roman bath house. Upstairs was more of the same: here a chasuble, there another bust, here one of those statues of Christ with a hole where his heart should be – and, in a glass case at the far end of the gallery, half a saint's leg. I didn't have my glasses, so I couldn't read the sign, but I assume it was half a saint's leg, for you'd only encase half of someone's leg in a specially made silver-and-glass foot-shaped container if he was a saint.

Half a leg in a glass container in a bejewelled glass box is unlikely to actually smell, but it seemed to give off the whiff you get from trays of pinned butterflies. Or maybe my imagination was running away with me. I don't know. I felt vaguely nauseous, left the museum quickly, found a café, sat outside with a view of a piazza, drank a coffee and checked my phone. No messages. Maybe Cora had woken up and decided I was a highly valued member of the Tread Lightly team. Who knows? If I really was unemployed, maybe this was the spur I needed to do the things I'd told myself I should do when I was doing the things that I used to do to avoid the things I should do. Or not. I ordered another coffee and closed my eyes.

DEATH IN NAPLES

Neapolitans have a sincere and willing interest in death. From the dead death of the saint's bones to the living death of the Camorra, they love the stuff. Any opportunity to give it expression and they take it, and nowhere is this on more appealing display than in the Cappella Sansevero. For here *The Dead Christ*, a sculpture that looks as if it has been carved from frozen yoghurt, is displayed in the middle of the chapel floor.

The figure itself was carved from alabaster and covered in a full-length shroud fashioned from a single piece of marble. The work is so skilled that the man's wounds can be seen through the marble, the dead veins on his forehead, the poor fingers – the burden, the misery and the tears. I took out my notebook and wrote:

In Naples, death is all around. It seeps from the pavements, the houses, the faces of the people you meet. And in the middle of February you can feel it in the cold wind that blows off the bay and swirls through the warren of streets of the centro storico. *Visit the Cappella Sansevero, a tomb chapel dedicated to death in all its forms, and you'll begin to understand the Neapolitan's fascination for the final joke. In the chapel itself, Giuseppe Sammartino's* Dead Christ *is probably the most mortal Christ you're ever likely to see, while if you take a turn around the crypt, you'll come across a pair of figures that predate (ref. German? bloke who plasticizes bodies and tours them etc. Think he's bald) by a couple of hundred years. Prepared by an 18-c. alchemist called Prince Raimondo (check name, seems like someone's taking the piss), his experiments on the human circulatory system earned him excommunication from the Church.*

What I didn't mention in my notes was one of the fabulous statues that watches over the dead Christ. Known as *Modesty*, she stands in marbled glory with a bewitching look on her face and a less than modest veil covering the most fabulous pair of breasts you're likely to see this side of anywhere. Modest? And I'm Swedish etc. But I hadn't had enough coffee – and I'd had an idea.

AN IDEA

I found a café, ordered coffee and called Daniel, my colleague who was covering the north. I say "colleague", but he was also my friend. I asked him where he was. He said: "Freezing my nuts off in Perugia."

I said: "Fancy a drink?"

"Where?"

"Rome?"

"I don't know. I was talking to Cora this morning. She's not happy."

"What was the problem?"

"You tell me, Matt. Sounds like it might be you, but then…"

"Come on, Daniel. Get on a train. I'll be in Rome this evening. We can meet in the morning, compare notes, check the gossip…"

"I'm meant to be in Assisi tomorrow."

"Forget Assisi. What is it? A big church and a load of pilgrims. Easy. Just frig the old copy and you're there."

"And is that what you've been doing? Frigging the old copy?"

"Come on, Daniel. Pasta on me. And a couple of German backpackers if we're lucky. You know… signed copies of the *Tread Lightly Guide*."

"You're not serious."

"No, Daniel. I used to be in Eric Clapton's backing band, but now I'm a Benedictine monk. Of course I'm not serious. But we can chew the fat, have a few drinks, you know... I'm staying at the Hotel Segreti. It's across the road from the Trevi Fountain." I let the idea hang for a moment. It twirled in the air like a hippy's garden chime. I heard its notes – its lovely notes. "I do need to talk."

"You always need to talk. All right – but one night, then I've got to get on with the job."

"Me too."

I heard a muffled laugh. "I'll text when I'm on the train."

"Sounds good to me," I said, and he hung up.

RAUTAVAARA

I caught an evening train to Rome. I had a comfortable seat with a clean window, quiet neighbours, and when the refreshment trolley came by, I bought a can of Orangina. While the man was looking for a cup, I reached down and palmed a small packet of pretzels from a cage at the bottom of the trolley. Then, when he'd moved on, I poured the drink, scribbled in my notebook, sipped, opened the pretzels, crunched, sipped some more, watched the view, scribbled some more, had a ten-minute snooze, woke up with the taste of aspartame in my mouth, poured some more and wrote…

If you really want to see Italy, there's no better way to travel than by train. Fast, efficient, clean and (usually) on time, the rail network offers the independent traveller an armchair view of the country. The pride of Trenitalia is the Frecciarossa, a bullet-type express that can carry you from Naples to Rome in around an hour. Splash out on First Class and you'll enjoy free drinks at your seat, which is comfortable enough to sleep in without waking up with a cricked neck (a tad personal here, watch that…)

When I arrived in Rome, I walked to the hotel. The streets were cold and dark, and drizzle was giving the pavements a dangerous slick, but I needed the walk. And it was all, as they say, copy.

Rome comes into its own on a winter's night. The bars and restaurants seem even more welcoming than ever, the floodlit monuments strangely unfamiliar, the sky an apocalyptic (?) shade of orange. The sound of a scooter echoes from five streets away, its noise made eerie by the hour, its headlight carving through the rain.

My hotel was a step away from the Trevi Fountain, but not close enough to be in the thick of the madness. When I asked for a top-floor room, the manager said that he didn't have such a thing, but mine was the best in the place, and he knew I'd enjoy my stay.

Hotel rooms. Everyone knows the score. I scored two out of ten. It was on the first floor, but the first floor turned out to be a cellar. I went up to go down. I noted the metaphor, opened the window and looked into a courtyard the size of a bath and as deep as a well. Feet passed by twenty feet above me. But optimism is the mother of need, so I closed the window and went to eat.

The trick with Italian restaurants (one trick) is to look for one where men in good scarves come to collect takeaway pizza. I found such a place in the street behind the hotel, stepped inside, shook the damp off my coat, dropped my umbrella in a bucket and ordered a Campari. I was warming up, relaxing into the possibility of making the best of a rather rum job, when my phone pinged. A text from Cora: "Where are you, ex-employee? On the plane yet?"

I texted: "I'm in Rome drinking Campari." I deleted the text. I texted: "I'm in Rome. Thought I'd finish the job anyway." I pressed "send", watched it fly and perused the menu. I chose *spaghetti alla carbonara* and a jug of white wine, sat back and observed my fellow diners.

Opposite me, an American couple were discussing investments. I decided they were doctors – he something to do with bones, she something to do with skin. On the far side of the room, a group of English men were drinking beer. They'd come to watch a game of rugby, and were making loud remarks about how they were going to stuff Italy out of sight and then find fat women. A husband and wife sat at the table next to me, ordered two glasses of wine and said nothing to each other. I couldn't work out where they were from, so after engaging them in small talk for a couple of minutes, I asked.

"Finland," he said.

"Ah," I said.

They drank.

I drank.

She said nothing.

I said: "The other day, I was listening to Rautavaara. His *Cantus Arcticus*. I love it…"

"Yes," he said.

"The birds, the melancholy…" and now I knew I should just shut up and wait for my food. The wife was squinting at me, and the husband was trying to decide what to eat. I pulled out my phone and stared at it. Cora hadn't texted back. The husband looked at me. He looked irritated. I put the phone away. My food arrived.

I'd been eating for five minutes, forking the pasta into my mouth and swilling it down with glasses of a battering wine, when he said: "We saw him."

"I'm sorry?"

"Rautavaara. He was in our town."

"Was he?"

"Yes. He has a good smile."

"I believe," I said, "Sibelius anointed him as his successor, so to speak. Not that anyone could really succeed Sibelius. Not in that sense…"

"No," said the husband, and then I sensed that that was it. I wasn't going to find out any more about Rautavaara. And I didn't. Their food arrived and, without another word, they began to eat.

HAIR

The drizzle turned to sleet and the sleet turned to snow. As I was heading back to my hotel, I stopped at a bar. It wasn't my usual sort of place. There was MTV on big screens, a pool table and bottles of flavoured vodka. It was still early and I was the first customer. I sat on a stool and when the barmaid asked what I wanted to drink I said, "Jack Daniels." She poured half a glass and pushed it towards me. I pulled out my notebook and scribbled something about snow. She leant across, watched me for a minute, did something with her hair and said: "What are you doing?"

"Working."

She laughed. "Working? That is work?"

"Yes."

"You're a writer?"

"Yes."

Once I'd have used this question – I'd have closed my notebook and come out with a line. I didn't come out with a line.

"What are you writing?"

"That depends."

"On what?"

"On my mood."

"So…" She reached over and tapped my notebook. She had thin fingers and a silver bracelet on her wrist. "What's your mood making you write now?"

"A guide book for tourists."

"About Rome?"

"About Italy."

"Italy? All of Italy? How can you write a book about all of Italy?"

"It's about the south."

"The south?"

"Yes."

"And you know the south?"

Saved by the phone. It pinged. A text from Daniel. "Arriving Rome Termini 16:35. Meet you there?"

"Sorry," I said to the barmaid. "I've got to take this."

"Sure," she said, and she went to do something out the back.

I texted: "See you there. I'll get you a room at my hotel. OK?"

He texted back: "Nice one. A domani. D."

"You got it."

I waited for a couple of minutes, watched my phone blink into silence and went back to my notebook.

Snow doesn't fall in Rome like it falls anywhere else. (Wrong. Don't pretend you're a poet.) Snow is different in Rome. Rome in the snow. When it snows in Rome, the streets fail in a way that snowed streets don't fail in the north. When it snows in Rome, the bars warm, the women huddle, the scooters stall, the men shout less loud. Snow. Rome. When it snows in Rome. When it snows in Rome, cigarettes become furnaces. When it snows. When it snows in Rome. When it snows and the flakes drift like dreams from another place, another place, another grief of ruins…

The barmaid came back. She'd tied her hair back and dabbed something on her lips. That's what she'd been doing. Her eyes were wide and brown. They were like nuts. I said: "I like your hair."

She said "Another?" and she pointed at my glass.

I tapped my fingers and said: "Thanks."

She poured.

She poured well. She poured like she needed feeding. She leant into the glass. She was good. I didn't complain. I said nothing. I looked at what I'd written, scratched a line through every word, snapped the notebook shut and put it in my pocket. "Nonsense," I said.

"Maybe you shouldn't write when you're drinking."

I thought about telling her that what I did when I drank was none of her business, but I didn't have the heart. She was only doing her job and I was trying to do mine, and we were the only people in the bar. We were the only people in Rome in the snow. She disappeared again. I fished in my pocket, pulled out the notebook and wrote:

When it snows in Rome, you can feel like the only person in the city, and however well you know the place, it will become a stranger to you. And if you find yourself in the warmth of a friendly place like Bar? (check name and hours) and you're offered the chance to toast your good fortune, then take it. For there are few places in the world where...

And now I didn't know what to say, but what the hell, it was a start. The glass went to the lips and the barmaid came back again. I thought about a story I knew, the famous one about the writer in the Parisian café, the clean place, well-lit and warm in the winter, and I thought about my story for kids. I looked at the notes I'd scribbled about Paris, the little boy, the kindly gentleman and the bird market. "Yes," I said, and I wrote the first paragraph. I waited a minute, read what I'd written and didn't cross it out. I put the notebook in my pocket and smiled, and when the barmaid asked me why I was smiling, I said: "Because sometimes I think I can do what I'm meant to do."

A COMFORTABLE MAN

In the morning, I was jaded. I opened the curtains and looked up at the grill that covered the well outside my window. I heard a yell and a crack and a curse. Someone had slipped on ice. I took a shower and went down for breakfast.

In those days, breakfast in a tourist hotel was almost always an erotic experience for me. As the women attacked the buffet, they moved fresh from a night of lust, fresh from the shower and fresh for another day of tramping the streets. They whispered to their men or whispered to their friends: whatever they did was enough to make me weep. I ate a pastry, drank coffee and headed out.

I'd planned to take a turn around a few of the sights, make notes and buy a pair of gloves, but as I was crossing the Palazzo Sciarra, I saw a poster: "The Renaissance in Rome. The inspiration of Michelangelo and Raphael. Sculptures, paintings and drawings from the Uffizi, the Hermitage, the Vatican, the Albertina, etc." I enjoy chewing on the Renaissance, so I gave the Palatine a miss, ducked into the museum and dropped my euros on the counter.

I'm a lucky man and I know it. So luck doesn't always come my way, and sometimes it prefers to spend time with other people, but that morning she waited for me with a smile on her face and took my hand before leading me on. For here was a gallery filled with 170 pieces by Michelangelo, Raphael, Perin del Vaga, Zuccari and the rest, all watched over by me, an old couple from Germany and the room attendants. And what rooms. The curators deserve a mention – Maria Grazia Bernardini and Marco Bussagli – for they had produced a show of such glory that when I reached the end I bought a cup of coffee, drank it quickly, turned around and did the whole thing again.

Two treasures shone above the rest. The first was Raphael's *Portrait of "Phaedra" Inghirami*. Scholar, poet, diplomat, librarian and favourite of popes and emperors, Signor Inghirami had a squint in his right eye and a well-fed look about his chubby face. His hat looked comfortable, and he held a pen over a blank sheet of paper. His left arm rested on an open book, and he had a thoughtful, faraway look in his good eye. His hat and coat were red, the folds in the cloth so real you could reach out and smooth them, his thumb ring tasteful, his inkwell full: here was a man you would have enjoyed meeting, a man whose taste in hats and literature and wine would have matched yours.

The second treasure was an unfinished statue by Michelangelo. Because no one knows if it represents David or Apollo, it's called *David/Apollo*. Some people can see the head of Goliath in the rock beneath the boy's foot, others see Apollo in the thoughtful gaze and perfect muscles. But what it's called is unimportant, for here are the marks of Michelangelo's chisel, and here is the place where the artist stepped back, shook his head, stopped work and walked away to do something else. I stood close enough to smell the marble and hear the weeping trapped in the stone, the trouble and pain and loss.

I should have been an art critic. When I was a kid, my father said I could be anything I wanted to be. All I had to do was put my mind to it. After my second turn around its glories, I left the exhibition, found a bar, sat at the table by the window, watched the snow and wondered if Raphael's mother and Michelangelo's father had said the same thing to their boys. And an hour later, as I sat in the taxi and rode to meet Daniel, I wondered if that's the sort of thing mothers and fathers have to say. But I wouldn't know. Maybe that was where I'd gone wrong. Maybe a kid would have given me something more than these scratchings. Like so many people, I know there are so many ways to go wrong in so little time.

MEETING AT THE STATION

As I walked down the freezing concourse of the Stazione Termini and ducked past the crowds of chanting rugby fans, I missed England. I missed the tattoos and piercings, the huddled girls walking winter streets with goose bumps on their milky cleavages, the boys in their tracksuits, the despair on middle-aged faces, Marks & Spencer, the scent of vinegar and bells, the broken pavements, the pinched mouths of the women, the fired eyes of the men and comfortable sound of complaint – the sweats smoking outside Wetherspoons, the clouds, the blackbirds and the rage – stopping to watch ambulances pass – collecting plates – watching rain and pretending to know something about wine – clouds – waiting.

I missed the courage and the mix, and everything being anything. England – I thought – is the only country in the world that isn't constrained by borders or sausage. Its national dress is a T-shirt and its culture is as old as ink – ink on the page, ink on fingers and especially ink under skin. I saw my ancestors when I thought about faces at home, the faces of the people who stood above the beach and showed their stamps and roared as the Romans landed. I saw the looks on the Romans' faces, the muttered "*Deus meus…*" the horror as the fleet floundered, the terror of the tide, the noise of the shingle, the twilight, the fires burning, the rumble of chariots, the shower of chalk rocks – the women baring their breasts, the men pissing from the cliffs, the dogs barking – the laughter as another ship tipped and split, the roar of wind and the fire.

I took out my notebook. It opened to the place where I'd ripped Cora's poem away. I could see the outline of the words impressed onto a blank page, so I traced over them and then did what poets do. I tinkered for twenty minutes. I changed the word "place" to the word "home" and then changed it back again, and by the time Daniel arrived, the poem was exactly as it was before I'd started tinkering.

He was wearing cord trousers, a check shirt, a grey jumper, a sensible coat, and was carrying a canvas bag. England in a man. He waved when he saw me. I waved back. The missing deepened. He said: "Bloody hell. Is there a match on?"

"Rugby," I said. "Italy England."

"Typical."

"Might be some copy in it."

"True."

"Maybe I'll write something about nationalism and send it to *The Guardian*."

"They'd love it."

"Or maybe I won't."

"That's more likely."

We took a cab to the hotel, and half an hour later we were in a bar where you could find a quiet corner table and talk beneath a photograph of smiling men holding fish. We sat with glasses in our hands and I said: "So how's it been?"

"Cold."

"Tell me about it."

"I was in Genoa on Wednesday. I had icicles on my nose. You've no idea…"

"I do," I said, and I told him about my apartment. I told him about my apartment and the single heater and Ravello, and I told him about Naples, and when he'd told me about Milan and Bologna we slipped into half a minute of reflective silence.

Daniel is a friend, but I don't know him all that well. He drinks slowly, and when he reaches his limit he starts talking about his wife, reminding himself that he misses her and wondering if it's too late to call her. I suppose you could say he's a romantic, but I wouldn't hold that against him. I wouldn't hold anything against him, even though he treats writing for Tread Lightly as a serious career. We talked some more about the job, reached a place where we couldn't find anything else to say, ordered some more drinks, and I said: "Did you speak to Cora?"

"Oh yes…"

"And what did she say?"

"Chris has gone."

"I know. And what did she say about me?"

"Nothing. Was she meant to?"

"I think I might have drunk too much in Naples. I called her when I shouldn't have…"

"So what did you say?"

"You don't need to know, but…"

"But what?"

"She fired me."

"She fired you?"

"Yes."

"Can you be fired over the phone?"

"I've no idea. Probably." I swirled my glass, shook my head and said: "You know what?"

"What?"

"I envy you."

He laughed. "You envy me?"

"Your certainty, your happiness, your wife…"

He laughed again, and we sank into a minute of silent thought. Then he said: "You know, I don't think you can be fired over the phone. You've got a contract?"

"Of course."

"Then she's got to give you eight weeks' notice, unless you're guilty of gross misconduct or something like that… Give her a call in the morning. You'll talk her round."

"I'm not sure about that," I said, and I went to get some more drinks.

We drank for another hour. I listened to him talk some more about Bologna, and he listened to me talk about Amalfi, and we talked about digital. He said our jobs would be redundant in a couple of years' time, maybe sooner. I said they'd always need people who could write. He said when people wanted recommendations and suggestions they went to their phones or their friends' blogs or the wikis. I said blogs were simply poorly focused photographs in words. He said "Yeah". I said: "The mania to write and take pictures is becoming a substitute for the actual experience. It's a form of pollution." And he said that when I put it like that, it was easy to agree. I said that whatever happened, the guide book would always have a role, and he said that anything was possible. I said it was impossible to touch your left elbow with your left hand. He said he'd break my arm to prove his point. I shook my head and we agreed there was no point talking any more about work, and we lapsed into a half-comfortable silence.

"I think it's time," he said.

"What for?"

"Bed."

"OK," I said. "I think I'll have a nightcap."

He stood up, pulled on his coat and ran a hand through his hair. "See you at breakfast?"

"I'll be there," I said.

ADRIANA

I sat at the bar. The barmaid poured me a drink, and while I admired its colour, she went to do something with her hair. When she came back she looked like a church. Her face was glowing and wings were growing from her back. Stained glass was in her eyes, and her ears were bells. I said I wanted to buy her a drink. She squinted at me, held my gaze for a moment and nodded. She turned, took a bottle off the shelf, poured herself a glass of something pale and sipped it. She asked who my friend was, and I told her. She looked like she'd been singing psalms. I thought about telling her I'd been to the desert. It was a quiet night in the bar, and the other drinkers were being served by her friends. There was no trouble there. Outside, the snow swirled, and the freezing air drifted like spent wishes. I felt tired. I was scratching to be let in. She smiled and poured me another drink. I put a fist of cash on the bar.

We made a deal.

She was the trumpet. I was the taxi. She was working late. I told her my name. Her name was Adriana. I told her I knew what her name meant. I heard a violin in my head. She told me she was a student of music. I said it didn't surprise me. I asked her if she wanted to come to the river. She asked me what I meant. I told her I'd show her. She told me she wanted to see. I asked her where she lived. She said: "I have to catch a bus." I told her I had a room in a hotel two minutes away. She asked me if I knew George Clooney. I told her he was a personal friend. She said: "You're lying." I said: "I am." She said "Now you're not..." and went to do something else with her hair.

When she came back, I asked her what instrument she was studying. She said: "The violin." I asked her if she'd been to Cremona. She said her family name was Amati. I asked her if it was true that her family had perfected the f-hole. She said "Yes", and the word came like a bridesmaid takes the final flower. I rolled away the stone. Her lips were wet.

I don't know.

I don't know if she joined me because she wanted to or because she didn't want to take the bus. Maybe she liked the sound of my hotel or the thought that she could lie in a wide bed in a basement on the first floor.

Did she need the bidding of sorrow? I have no idea, but she took my arm and walked with me and let me push the door for her and followed me to my room, and while I brushed my teeth she showered, and while I showered she brushed her teeth, and when I was dry she was lying between my sheets.

"What did you mean..." she said, "about coming to the river?" I said "I don't know", and she shook her head, put her hand on my chest and told me that I couldn't make love with her, but it would be all right to sleep with her. I told I that I couldn't make love with her anyway, and she asked me if that was because I was old, and I said "Yes".

I woke up in the night. I looked at my phone. It was half-past three. I had no idea where I was. It took me a few minutes and then I remembered. I turned to look at her. She was asleep. Her face was turned towards the wall. She breathed. Her chest rose, held its place like a cat at a cliff and then it fell. I moved and held my hand over her face. I felt her breath. It was warm. I smelt my hand. It smelt of oregano. I looked towards the window. I saw the shadow of snow drifting against the curtains. I heard water dripping in the bathroom – a car in the street – someone walking by – a siren.

I lay down again, pulled the sheets and blankets up, and put my hand on her arm. She whispered a name. I left my hand where it was. I thought about Cora, saw the guitar she never played resting against the corner of her bedroom wall, the picture of Paris in her kitchen, the smell of her neck, the taste of her skin. I whispered her name and, as the word turned in the air, I knew. I knew as deeply and finally as I'd known anything in my life – like the dog that chases the car or the bridge that crosses the torrent – I knew we had no choice. Some people say "Never go back" – but some people don't know what they're talking about.

ADRIANA LEAVING

I woke again, this time to the sound of feet. The bathroom light came on. I heard the sound of water. Adriana came out and padded around the bedroom. She had a light body. I pretended to be asleep. I watched her bend and pick up her socks. As she moved, she left the scent of cinnamon and paint in the air. She pulled on her pants and palmed her breasts into her bra, folded her shirt over her shoulders, stepped into her trousers and fastened her belt.

She picked up her bag and stood in the middle of the room, checked she had everything and turned towards me. She reached out and I felt her hand on the bed. Then she bent and kissed my forehead. I moved, as if to wake. She said "Sleep…" and then she picked up her shoes, went to the door, opened it, stepped out, closed it, and I listened as her feet padded down the corridor. I turned over and pulled the pillow she'd used towards me, and buried my face in it.

I wasn't sentimental or romantic, and I had no desire. All I wanted to do was talk to the woman I was missing. I waited until Adriana's scent had failed and then I fell asleep.

I had a dream. I was the man who banged the drums on a slave galley. I wore a loin cloth and leather straps that crossed in the middle of my chest. Each oar was operated by two men who were roped together. One man pulled the oar forward and the other man pulled it back. Between each stroke, the man who wasn't pulling was flipped into the air and dashed across the deck. This resulted in mayhem and death, and every couple of minutes a man with a whip would cut a dead man from the ropes that bound him and throw the body into the sea. I asked the captain why the galley wasted so many men when all we had to do was rearrange the way the oars were pulled. The captain said: "Are you questioning my wisdom?" I said: "Of course not. I'm just concerned." The captain called to the man with the whip and said: "Throw the drummer over the side." The next thing I knew I was in the water, surrounded by the bobbing heads of the dead and dying. Gulls were circling, pecking at eyes and bellies. The galley headed towards the horizon. I heard a voice say "Swim", and then I heard a howling. I woke up. The howling carried on for a moment, then stopped. I'd woken myself up. I got out of bed, checked my phone and went to the bathroom. I put my back against the wall and slipped to the floor. I sat there, my knees tucked to my chin, and took deep, long breaths. Then, after half an hour, I had a shower and went down for breakfast.

BREAKFAST WITH DANIEL

Daniel was sitting at a table with a cup of coffee and a pastry. I fetched a cup of tea and a bowl of fruit and sat opposite him. He said: "Good night?"

"Not bad," I said, and I ate a piece of pineapple.

He drank some coffee and said: "Remind me why you asked me to meet you."

"We haven't seen each other for a while, and I thought it might be a good idea to talk about the job. Compare notes, you know…"

"No, I don't know," he said.

"Has it been going OK?"

"Has what been going OK?"

"The job."

"OK isn't a word I use."

I speared an apricot and said: "Daniel, are you always this grumpy in the morning?"

"You call this grumpy?"

"All you had to do was say no."

"To what?"

"To coming to Rome."

"True. Have you seen the forecast?"

"No."

"There's going to be six inches of snow. And I'm meant to be in Assisi."

"You'll get there. Don't worry."

"Your confidence does not inspire, Matt," he said, and he went to get some more coffee.

When he came back, he took a deep breath and said: "So, what are you doing today?"

"I've got an afternoon train to Atrani. And I suppose I should talk to Cora."

"That might be a good idea. You should apologize. Throw yourself at her mercy."

"Oh God…"

"Do it, Matt. And I'll give you some advice for nothing."

"Go on then."

"Get back together…"

I laughed.

"I mean it. You might not think it, but you're made for each other. Everyone says so."

"Do they?"

"Yes."

"And what else do they say?"

"Not a lot. Most people have better things to talk about than you."

"We get back together?"

"Yes."

"And how do you propose I achieve this?"

"I don't know. Tell her she's beautiful and you were a fool?"

"She already knows that."

"Take her away for a weekend…"

"Like that's going to happen."

"OK. Give her something. Give her something that tells her what she means to you."

"Advise me, Daniel. Tell me…"

"I don't know. What does she like?"

"Beautiful things. Rare things…"

"Then buy her something beautiful. Something beautiful and rare."

"Like what?"

"I don't know. Use your imagination."

"I'm hopeless at buying presents," I said, and I was reminded of something, a success I achieved in my time with her, but before I could take the memory any further, a pair of women appeared, walked to the breakfast buffet, stared at the food and shook their heads. They looked like sisters. I watched them for a couple of minutes and almost asked Daniel if he had any thoughts about the eroticism of the tourist breakfast experience, but I stopped myself. He was squinting at his half-eaten pastry, and there was nothing I could do to change his mood. "OK," I said. "I'll do it."

"You'll do what?"

"I'll buy her a present."

"Good man," he said, and he went to get a banana.

THE MOST BEAUTIFUL
OBJECT IN THE WORLD

I recalled another time, a time when no one thought about what had passed away. The dove was free, and Cora and I had been seeing each other for a year. I suggested we celebrate. When she asked me what sort of celebration I had in mind, I told her I wanted to show her the most beautiful object in the world. When she asked me what this was, I told her to pack her passport and a bag of clothes – and, if she wanted, a book.

We took the Eurostar to Paris, ate a good lunch in the 10th and caught a sleeper to Munich.

"Munich?" she said.

I said, "Yes."

"Why? What's in Munich?" she said, and I said, "Wait and see…" and we ate cheese and drank a bottle of wine in the restaurant car and then went to our cabin, snuggled down in the bunks and let the train rattle us through the night.

The most beautiful object in the world sits in a glass case in the Treasury of the Palace of the Kings of Bavaria, the Munich Residenz. The "Palatine Crown", made around 1370 for Queen Anne, wife of King Richard II, is the oldest surviving English crown jewel. Twelve free-standing gold lilies – six small, six taller – grow from a hinged circle, the edges of the leaves detailed with tiny frills – or are they nicks? Details, details. Everything is detail. Each lily is set with sapphires, rubies, emeralds and diamonds cut *en cabochon*; pearls decorate the rest – some singly, some in groups of four. It's a medieval miracle, and if you put your ear as close to the case as you can, you'll hear songs drifting from the gold, and sighs from the pearls. The emeralds whisper, and the rubies tell a story about the hair that drifted in their glow. The sapphires hold secrets and the diamonds wink. It's as cruel as an object can be, and as perfect. The first time we stood in front of it, Cora was quiet for five minutes, then said: "You're right. It is."

I don't believe objects have the power to influence behaviour simply by existing, but the crown gave me something. I reached out and took Cora's hand, and squeezed it.

"What's it doing here?"

I explained that the English medieval crown jewels had been destroyed in the Civil War, melted down, broken up, stolen by bishops and whores. "Except for this. It came as part of the dowry of Henry IV's daughter when she married into the house of Wittelsbach, and it's stayed here ever since."

"You could be a guide."

"And you could give me a tip."

We stayed in Munich for a couple of days. Every morning, we'd have breakfast and walk to the Residenz, circle the crown for an hour and then stroll to a café for coffee. And every morning we'd see something new in the thing, some detail – the budding leaves on the stem of the lilies, the hidden hinges in the ring, the symbols on the ring, the piercing of the pearls, the way the whole looked vaguely lopsided. Cora wondered what colour Queen Anne's hair was. I said I didn't know, but imagined she was a redhead – and I said I could become obsessed with it. She then said: "Sometimes, when you look at it, you look like you're in love."

On our last morning, as we circled it and watched the colours fly, I leant towards her and whispered: "Shall I steal it for you?"

"Could you?" she said.

"Probably not," I said. "But I've always wanted to steal something precious."

"Why?"

"Just to see if I could. I'd keep it for a few days and then give it back."

"You're crazy," she said.

"You're beautiful," I said.

"And so are you," she said, "in a way."

"Thanks."

"And thank you," she said, "for showing me the most beautiful object in the world."

A NEW MUSIC

After breakfast I said goodbye to Daniel, watched him disappear towards the station, and then I walked through the freezing streets to the Spanish Steps. Workmen were sweeping snow. Some Japanese tourists were standing in a huddle. Their guide was telling them something about Francesco de Sanctis. They looked cold and bewildered, and some of them were wearing small rucksacks in the shape of cats. I felt cold and bewildered too: my shoes were soaked and my nose was blue. I found a bar, ordered a coffee, sat at a window table and took out my notebook. I found a pen and held it over a page.

I was wondering about arrogance and hypocrisy and Tread Lightly and aeroplanes. I watched vapour trails in the sky, smelt baking in the morning air, and thought about cheese omelettes. I like cheese. Someone had left a copy of an English newspaper on the table. I picked it up and read an interview with a novelist who talked about climate change, about how it was everyone's responsibility to think about their responsibilities, and how writers are the guardians of the planet's conscience. And how when she drove from her house in London to her cottage in the country, she was overwhelmed by the weight of the burden she was carrying. "We," she wrote, "are on the cusp. Our eyes are closed. We're walking towards a cliff, and no one knows what's over the edge." I remembered Frank Leahy and his wisdom:

"Egotism is the anaesthetic that dulls the pain of stupidity" – and I thought that if the novelist wanted to try suicide, all she'd have to do was jump off her own ego. Artists are actors before they're artists, and actors are never artists. I said "Cheese…" to the paper, folded it into quarters, stuffed it into a gap between the table and the wall and ordered another coffee.

Was there any hope? There was. People are marginal. People are one species. There are over eight and a half million species on the planet. When the novelist's car has helped destroy her environment and half the species that live in it, and once she's flown back from a weekend in NYC, over four million species will survive. And then they will build a world even she – at the rage of her powers – could never imagine. They will invent a new music, their languages will sound like metal and their wars will blind Mars. Their thousand eyes will glow red and flowers will grow from copper.

Sometimes my ramblings amazed me. They were bigger than the sea. The waves broke. The shingle sang. My phone pinged. I pulled it from my pocket. I stared at it. Cora had sent a text. A single question mark hung in the poison of indium tin oxide, drifted for a moment and then faded away.

HANGING WORDS

I called her. I said, "Cora?"

"Matt. Where are you?"

"Rome."

"Rome? You're meant to be in London. What are you doing there?"

"Working."

"Who for?"

"You."

"I'm sure I fired you. Let me check." I heard the sound of rustling paper. "Yes. I did. You're unemployed."

"And I think you'll find," I said, slowly now, "that I have a contract to complete this project…"

"And I think you'll find," she said, "that a clause in your contract states it may be cancelled at any time should your employer consider your behaviour breaches any of the terms of your original contract of employment."

I stared at my coffee. I listened to the sound of her breathing. It sounded like a bird flying into a window, over and over and over again.

"Cora…"

"Yes?"

"I apologize. I shouldn't have said what I said. I was drunk and I was a fool."

"Correction. You *are* a fool."

"I'm a fool," I said, "but I do have some good copy."

"Says who?"

"Well… Daniel seemed to think it was OK."

"Daniel? What's he got to do with anything?"

"He read it."

"When?"

"We spent the evening together."

"I thought he was in Assisi."

"He is now. Or should be. Don't have a go at him. I invited him down. I wanted to compare notes."

"And get him on your side?"

"No fear of that."

"I like Daniel."

"I know."

"He's a good judge of character. He's honest, dependable, sober. And he can write the balls off a horse."

"I can write the balls off two horses."

"And he's modest. He listens…"

"So he's everything I'm not."

"I didn't say that."

"But you thought it."

"Any insecurities you have, Matt, are of your own making."

"I'm proud of my insecurities, Cora."

"Interesting."

I let the word hang. I like hanging words. I looked at my shoes. They needed polish. I had no idea about polish. How was it made? Where did it come from? Who made it?

"Look," I said. "I was out of order. I'm going on the wagon."

"And what wagon would that be? The brewer's dray? The whisky man's dog cart?"

"Please. I'm struggling here." As the words came out, I surprised myself, but what the hell. There was nothing I could do about my mouth. I'd never said I was struggling to anyone. This was new to me. "I'm really struggling…"

"With what?'

"With everything."

"Everything?"

"Yes?"

"Please don't tell me you mean what I think you mean."

"Everything is everything, Cora."

"God, Matt – the bullshit. Sometimes it amazes even me."

"It astonishes me…"

I heard tapping – her pen on the desk. She tapped her pen on her desk when she was irritated. "OK," she said. "Seeing as we're halfway through this project, you can finish it. But when you get back we're taking a walk."

"Deal."

"No, Matt, I'm the one who says 'deal'."

"OK."

A SPECIAL GIFT

I left the café and strolled to the north side of the Piazza di Spagna. I wasn't looking for anything. I was calm and thinking about something else. I was thinking about the time I smoked a cigarette. I was fifteen, it was a Saturday afternoon and I'd met some school friends at the Angel. We were doing the things schoolboys do on a bored Saturday afternoon – hanging around telephone boxes and outside chip shops. Someone suggested we sit on the benches on Islington Green and toss stuff at the pigeons, and while we were there someone else took out a packet of cigarettes, flicked one out and passed them around. I said "Ta", like I knew what I was doing and had been doing it for years, and took a light and my first drag. I didn't inhale, and the others laughed and said: "You got to take it down, Matt. Swallow it."

"I know."

"Go on then."

That first lungful hit me hard, and as my head began to white out and I slid down the bench, my friends laughed again. I was sitting on the grass when I took my second drag, and then I was sick. Someone – I call all these friends "someone" because even though I have a memory of Mick, Nigel, Spencer and Greg, I couldn't say for sure who was who – someone said: "You've got stuff on your shirt…" and I was sick again.

"Nice," said someone else, and I said, "Yeah. I'll get used to it in a minute."

"Course you will."

I was thinking about this afternoon and North London and wondering if I should move back to that part of the city, and I was wondering what had happened to my school friends, when I saw a small antique shop. It was tucked into the corner of the square. It had a red door and a small window. I suppose some things are meant to happen, or at least could be meant to happen. I didn't know. My mind was slow. I stood for a few minutes, my hands in my pockets, looking at the objects in the window. An oil painting of Christ calming the waters (Roman school by an unknown hand, late seventeenth century) on an easel, and a pair of walnut-and-papier-mâché globes, one on each side of the painting. I cupped my hands, pressed against the glass and saw rare and beautiful things hanging on the walls and sitting in glass cabinets. I took a deep breath, pushed a bell by a brass nameplate and a moment later a gentleman in a black suit unlocked the door and let me in. He stood back to let me step inside and asked if I was looking for anything in particular. I told him I was, but didn't know exactly what.

"I'm looking for a special gift," I said.

"I see," he said.

"Yes."

"Everything we have could be a special gift," he said, and he spread his arms.

"Something small, I think," I said.

"It is for a woman?"

"Yes."

"Of course." He gave me a small, knowing smile and said: "Then I can find you a brooch? Or maybe a ring?"

"I think a brooch. But if you have a ring…" I said.

"I'm sure we might have the very thing you're looking for." He touched my arm. "Let me show you," he said, and he led the way.

The front of the shop was small, but inside it was enormous. Small galleries opened off a central corridor, and more galleries led from these. One contained seventeenth-century French furniture, another nineteenth-century Italian watercolours, another Roman antiquities, another eighteenth-century statuary. The smell of polish and cigars drifted in the air, and the sound of ticking clocks. There was a reverential atmosphere, like in a church or in the moment before a conductor raises his baton. "Here," said the gentleman, and he showed me into a room where glass cases and cabinets lined the walls. "I'm sure you'll find something that will make her fall in love with you all over again."

I was going to ask him how he knew, but I bit my tongue. I kept quiet. I was a mouse under the floor.

"Very special things," he said. "Please take your time." He pointed to a bell push on the wall. "And if you wish to see something in your hands, please use this."

"Thank you," I said, and he left me to myself.

I looked at everything. Some of the objects were ugly – a horrific cameo sticks in my mind – some were gaudy, and some looked plain wrong, but here and there were things of such beauty that they stopped me. And when I saw a gold brooch in the shape of a cat playing with a ball of wool, I knew I'd found it. It wasn't the most beautiful object in the world, but it was close. The animal's eyes were tiny jewels, and the ball of wool shimmered – and the thing was so perfect, so delicate, I felt a lump in my throat. What had I said to Daniel? "I'm hopeless at buying presents." I saw myself giving it to Cora. I saw the look in her eyes as she saw it for the first time. I saw it pinned to her best jacket, and I saw her fingers as they traced the curve of the back, the gems, the lovely curl of the tail. I went to the bell, pressed it, and a minute later the gentleman appeared at my shoulder and said: "You have found something?"

"I think I have." I pointed at the brooch. "Can I see it?"

"You have an excellent eye." He took a bunch of keys from his pocket, opened the case, took the brooch out, carried it to a desk, laid it on a velvet mat and said: "This is English. 1880, we think. Gold, of course, with a silver clasp. The eyes are emerald, and the ball of wool is a pearl. Flawless."

I held my hand over it. I was warm. "May I hold it?"

"But of course."

I picked it up. It was heavier than I'd expected, and had been worked so finely that it could have been transformed from a real cat by some miraculous process that blinded its discoverer. I held it to the light, watched its lambent glow and its blinking gems. I stroked its back and I thought I heard it purr. I did – I heard it purr.

"How beautiful is it?" I said.

The gentleman looked at me, shook his head and said: "Is that a question?"

"Not really. How much is it?"

"One minute." He opened one of the desk's drawers, took out a small black book and leafed through the pages. "Yes," he said. "An unusual English Victorian brooch in the shape of a playful cat. Eighteen-carat yellow gold, two round cut emeralds, a single natural pearl. 1880. This will be 1,200 euro."

I nodded but didn't say anything. The gentleman didn't know if I could afford it or if I was out of my depth. He said: "Is it what you were looking for?"

"It is," I said. "Exactly."

"Your friend will like it?"

"She'll love it."

I turned it over in my hand and rubbed my thumbs over the emeralds.

"Love," he said, "is all there is in a gift. The money – it means nothing."

"That's true."

"Maybe you need some time to think?"

"Is that a question?"

He raised his eyebrows. "It is."

"I think I do," I said, and I put the brooch back on the velvet.

"Please. Take as much time as you need."

I nodded.

"We open at half-past ten every morning," said the gentleman as he walked me to the door. "You're most welcome to come and look again."

"Thank you," I said, and he led me away from the room and down the corridor, and as we stood at the street door, we shook hands and he gave me a look that started at sympathy, dived into pity and stayed there. I looked down – I saw the pity – it was flipping in shallow water. It didn't think it could drown but it was wrong. Pity. A lost emotion. A middle name that's never used. A cheese in a fridge that was switched off last month.

IRRATIONAL

It was half-past one when I left the antique shop. It was lunch-time, but I wasn't hungry. I walked through the back streets to the river, over the Ponte Sant'Angelo and around the castle walls. I thought about buying a ticket and climbing the bricked circles to the roof, but I'd done that, written about it, stood on the top walls and looked towards the Vatican. I'd stared at the dome and the crowds, and I'd heard the bells.

I bought a cup of coffee from a stall and sat to drink and watch the hawkers. The world was selling, and every time I managed not to think about the brooch for a couple of minutes, a couple of minutes was all it was. I told a man in a blue hat that I didn't want a neon light stick or a collection of twelve postcards, and walked back the way I'd come. I was going back to the hotel for my bag. My train was at half-past four. I was going back to the hotel, but when I reached the Piazza di Spagna, I stepped into a bar and bought a glass of wine. I thought about money. I had £340 in my current account and £2,600 in a deposit account, and more in some other accounts.

I've been irrational. In addition to the stealing and the drinking, I could list other ways and times. Once I flew from London to Islay because I had a sudden wish to visit the Laphroaig distillery, and I spent the following three days in a frosted daze in a dark B&B in Port Ellen. Another time I paid £125 for a signed first edition of W.S. Graham's *Implements in Their Places* because I'd drunk four pints and found myself in a shop by the British Museum. And then there was the time I gave my sister an eighteenth-century Neapolitan bowl-back mandolin I found in a junkshop. My sister is a difficult person to love, but love – can it ever be rational? And can a mandolin ever be less than beautiful? And can a woman like Cora be anything less than beautiful?

There's a moment in everyone's life when you realize the truth, and you realize that the truth can never set you free: it can only bind you like Prometheus – and when I say this I'm not drifting into pretension, for Prometheus is exactly who is bound here. A good man who stole a precious thing, showed his fists to the gods and took his punishment, always looking for the best, aiming for genius.

I ordered another glass of wine. I held it up. The sun caught its colour and flashed against my skin. I thought about Cora's skin. I thought about the way she would lie on her stomach in a Saturday-morning bed, the sheet pulled back because she was too hot. I smelt her scent in the air, the scent from the top of her head and the crease behind her elbow. She could have been sitting next to me. I drank. The wine tasted better than the air. Everything in the world was better for Rome, and all doubt slipped away, and something like the obvious stepped into its place, slipped a jacket off its shoulders and smiled at me.

POCKET

I didn't expect it, but in the way that desire came down as I drank, peace put its hands on me as a mother might lay hands on her child's head. The child looked up, the mother looked down; the peace layered and drifted like mist over a shallow valley. I could have put my hand in the mist and mixed it like a sauce, or I could have swept a bottle over its surface and kept some for ever.

I crossed the square to the antique shop. I'd felt the first finger of love, and I wanted to see the golden cat again. I wanted to fix its image in my mind so that one day I could describe it to Cora. I wanted to smell the scents of polish and cigars, and feel the quiet and respect. I rang the bell, and the same gentleman opened the door. He smiled when he saw me, said "Welcome back, sir" and stood to one side. I stepped inside. "You've made a decision about the brooch?"

"Not exactly," I said. "I'll need to speak to my bank before I do that, but I would like to see it again."

"Of course. Please. Follow me."

As we walked, the gentleman fiddled with his cufflinks, touched the knot in his tie and said, "I had the feeling you would return today, even if it wasn't to buy."

"I'm sorry," I said, "but I couldn't get it out of my mind. It was starting to haunt me, I think."

"You have no need to apologize, sir. I understand exactly how you feel."

We reached the room and stepped up to the case, and he unlocked it, took the brooch to the desk, laid it on the velvet, and I said: "I know I only saw it for five minutes, and I know this will sound like the sort of thing people say to you every day, but I feel like I've known it all my life."

His deference was holy. "Please. Take more than five minutes. Take all the time you need…"

"Thank you," I said, and while he went to another corner of the room and started to rearrange a collection of porcelain figures, I picked up the brooch and ran my fingers over the emeralds and the beautiful pearl. I held it to my nose: it smelt like a drawer in an old wardrobe. I put it to my ear. I heard it purr again, and then – a telephone ringing. It was an old-fashioned ring. I was taken back to my childhood home, the huge phone on the hall table in the dark hall, the one I was forbidden to touch – the hushed voice when my father answered it – the whispered words as he spoke to whoever it was he was talking to – the solid clunk as the receiver was put back on its cradle. The gentleman stepped away from the porcelain, gave me a small bow, looked straight into my eyes, said "Please excuse me" and left the room. I heard his footsteps as he walked down the corridor; a door opened, the telephone stopped ringing. His muffled voice carried back to where I was. I couldn't hear what he was saying. I couldn't hear what I was thinking. I couldn't hear anything at all. I breathed on the brooch, polished it on my sleeve and looked at the ceiling. I wasn't looking for cameras – not that I saw any. I wasn't looking for anything. I put the brooch back on the desk, took a step away and caught my reflection in the glass of a case of silver goblets. I stared at myself. I hadn't shaved for a few days. I didn't need to talk to my bank. I could afford the brooch. I watched my hand reach out for it. I picked it up without looking at it, turned it over in my hand. It slipped into my palm. I closed my eyes. I saw Cora. I saw Cora's face when she saw the brooch, and I saw her pinning it on her jacket. I saw her smiling. I opened my eyes. The gentleman was still talking in another room. I said "Do you want to come with me?" to the brooch, and it purred. It dropped into my pocket. I took another step from the desk, turned away and walked out of the room. I walked down the corridor to the front door. As I passed the room where the gentleman was talking, I saw him. He was standing with his back to me, listening to whoever was talking. I could have walked on, could have slipped out of the door and not looked back, twisted into the city and faded into a doorway. But I didn't. I took the cat out of my pocket and stepped into the room. The gentleman said "Ciao", put the phone down and turned to look at me. I opened my hand, put the cat on a table and said: "I want this."

"I know you do."

"Can you keep it for me?"

"For how long?"

"I have to leave Rome today, but I'll be back in a week."

"A week?"

"Yes."

He looked deep into my eyes and nodded. "A week, and then I will put it back on show. But meanwhile, it stays here…" and he stepped to a walnut bureau, opened a small drawer and placed it inside.

"Thank you."

"Of course," he said, and he gave me a business card and walked me to the door. The card read *Antichità Buonarroti, Piazza di Spagna. Roma*. I said: "And you are Signor Buonarroti?"

"I am."

"Matthew Baxter," I said, and I held out my hand.

"A pleasure, Signor Baxter," he said, and we said goodbye and I stepped into the square, turned right and walked away. I headed for a side street, then into an alley that led towards a wider road. There was traffic here – cars and bikes. I crossed the road, and when I was on the other side, I stopped and looked back towards the shop. Once I had been a thief. Now I was just a man with an idea, and ten minutes later I was sitting on my hotel bed.

LA PETITE MORT

I suppose I should have sealed my desire by paying a deposit for the brooch. Ten per cent? What would that be? 120 euro. I had that in my pocket. And I suppose I could say I was trapped in a beautiful existential jail, its perfect bars singing with a perfect song, its walls running with mist, its floor cold and hot in equally absurd measures.

I had an hour to catch my train. I was going back to Atrani. I returned to my hotel, picked up my bag, paid the bill, said goodbye to the receptionist, stepped into the street and started walking. I felt a curious lightness, and a gap between the reality of what I had almost done in the shop and the reality of what I had done. I examined this gap as I walked, and it became a sort of waking dream that left the weight of the brooch in my pocket and a film of light guilt. And this guilt translated itself into my gait. People could change – someone had told me this – and sometimes for the better. But did they change instantly or slowly? Slowly seemed more likely, like advancing ice, but did it matter as long as the change was for the better? My head dropped – I kept to the sides of buildings – I moved quickly and didn't look at anyone or stop when someone asked for change. It was a cold night, and the streets were beginning to freeze again, so I wasn't the only one walking in a huddle, and when I reached the station I wasn't the only one in a hurry to find a train. I was in my seat with ten minutes to spare, and settled with my head against my coat. I closed my eyes and dozed for a moment, and then the train jolted and started to pull away. I opened my eyes and watched people on the platform waving and walking away. The tiny nap had made me light-headed, vaguely empty and post-something. Coital? Maybe. Whatever. A few flakes of snow were drifting in the air, and by the time we reached the edge of town we were travelling through a blizzard. Half an hour later, the snow was gone and we were heading into a dry evening.

THE CORNICHE AT NIGHT

The train was late arriving in Salerno. I stood in the twilight and cold outside the station, and waited for a bus. I waited three quarters of an hour. I saw drunks, whores, three frightened children and a pair of bored policemen. Orange clouds bled into the west; the sky darkened and, as I watched, a cloud of starlings appeared. At first they were quiet and ordered and disappeared behind some trees, but then they started to do the thing starlings sometimes do, swirling and cupping and balling, diving in strings behind the roof of the station, flowing back and around, deepening and finding their way into another string. Clouds of smoke, pillars of dust, tumbles of water. People took out their phones to film the birds and screamed as they came close and headed back the way they'd come.

I'd seen a film of starlings doing this over a field in Somerset. They're creating mathematical chaos, apparently. Larger shapes created by an endless variety of smaller shapes, designed without thought to fool predators. This is what the commentary said – "without thought" – but who's to say? I was in a quiet and contemplative mood, and was ready to believe that the birds had a collective consciousness, or were a reflection of my mind, or a sign from the world or a sign from Cora. Everything – I thought – could be a sign from Cora, or even a message.

As I got on the bus, the birds were still murmuring, and as I slipped my headphones on they appeared to fly in time, rhythm and sight with the tune I was listening to. And then we were away and onto the road that led through the edge of town to the coast road and home.

I'd missed Cora before, but never like this. I wanted her to be sitting next to me on the bus, I wanted to point out a bakery where I'd bought a bag of good pastries, and I wanted to hear her gasp as we took the first bend on the coast road. As we dropped into the town of Cetara, I wanted to tell her all about the anchovy boats and the beardy men who motored out to the fishing grounds with their nets and cigarettes, and when we rounded the corner at the western edge of Minori and the lights of Ravello appeared, I needed to point to Gore Vidal's house and whistle through my teeth. And I wanted to put my hand in my pocket and take out the brooch I hadn't bought and show it to her. I wanted her eyes to widen at the sight of its golden back and the emeralds and the grit of the pearl. And I wanted her to lean towards me and kiss me and thank me and whisper a little prayer in my ear.

Some people believe a prayer is a gift. Others say it's a cry, or a stable in the field where flocks of words graze – or a shopping list – or a way of whispering to the impossible – a song to a life lost or a meal never eaten. My thoughts on the subject change with the seasons: sometimes I think a prayer is an admission of failure and loss – our failure to have any control over events at all, our loss of control. We can't change things by closing our eyes and muttering. We can't see beyond the edge. We are all bald. There is no such thing as fate. Blood is red, hair falls, dogs appear mysteriously in school playgrounds, feet fail, organs die. Then I think a prayer is a true expression of love and communication, a way of reaching towards an understanding of the improbable. We are all beautiful, fate is as tangible as thought, and we are more than a bundle of future memories.

I believe these things all at once and at the same time, so I did allow myself to say a dozen words to the dark, to memories and the idea that if I could change I would change, and the trumpet in my head would find its pitch before the piano tuner left. And as the bus clipped the last kerb and Atrani appeared below me, I imagined a light burning in my apartment, two glasses on the table and a single hanging note. I closed my eyes and saw Cora sitting in the kitchen reading a book, a half-smile on her face. I opened my eyes. The bus stopped. I stood up. The driver opened the door. I stepped onto the pavement. I let the bus leave. I was alone with the gulls and the wash of the sea, and the church bell struck the hour.

My apartment was colder than ever, and as I stood in the kitchen and stared at a single apple in a bowl, I listened to the sea drag the shingle across the beach. I took a bottle of wine from the fridge, poured a glass and sat to watch lights blink through the night. I hadn't taken off my coat or my hat, and as my breath steamed and the wine started to do its work, I closed my eyes and let my other senses do the bidding.

COLLISION

If the Palatine Crown is the most beautiful object in the world, and its sweet gems are thieved eyes from a cave of queens, then the brooch in the Roman antique shop was the second most beautiful object in the world. In my heart I knew this wasn't true, but something kept nagging me, and told me it was beyond reason or belief. Like one of those shafts of sunlight you might snatch on a late-autumn evening, or the song of a nightingale caught in the middle of a sleepless August night, or the touch of a lover's fingers on your back in a room overlooking a sleepy river, or the scent of a peat fire drifting over a windy garden, or the taste of fresh mozzarella, or the thought that people you admire are coming to dinner, or the knowledge that you will wake beside the only woman you ever really knew, or… or. I pictured the brooch, remembered the feel of it as I ran my fingers over the tip of its tail, over its back, down to the nape of its neck and over its little ears. I remembered its emerald eyes and the pearl of wool and the imagined purr, the light refracted and the beauty of its gold and its age. I opened my eyes, reached for my glass, sipped, took out my notebook and ran my fingers over a blank page. I picked up a pen, made some squiggles in the corner of the page and tried to do what I was paid to do.

It's said that the road from Salerno to Sorrento is one of the most beautiful in Europe, maybe even the most beautiful in the world (what about that one in Dorset where I drove a Toyota into a ditch?). Aficionados insist that the only way to travel this corniche is in a vintage convertible – the roof down, jazz on the radio, elbow resting on the sill, the wind in your hair, your destination a restaurant on a bluff run by a smart young chef and his mother. And although there is an undeniable attraction to this approach, I would suggest that the best way to travel it is by bus as a February sun is setting. In summer, the road is impossible – a continual, slow-moving traffic jam, but in the winter it's yours. And with a seat by the window and a good driver looking after the twists, turns and tunnels, the journey feels like a pilgrimage to the heart of something Proustian, a place where memory and thought and geography collide in a perfect mélange of… (bollocks).

Once Salerno is left behind, the road climbs slowly, and the first of the precipitous houses and hotels that dot the coast appear. But it's only when you pass Capo d'Orso that its full magnificence is revealed. Sheer cliffs drop into the inky sea, bluffs and crags hang over the road, the regular blare of the driver's horn becomes the metronome of your passage, suicidal scooter riders overtake on blind bends, the netted lemon groves rise and fall on every side (check that net business. Why?)

Cetara, a quiet little fishing village, famous for its anchovies, offers a first taste of the coast's delights and (fill in here) as you wind your way through the narrow streets, it's tempting to stop and sample the pleasures of one of the many restaurants that hide in its shuttered back streets…

"No," I said. "Forget it." The words bounced off the walls. My stuff was reading like a blog. Maybe it *was* a blog. Weren't blogs the future of travel writing? That's what someone had said at the last meeting I'd been required to attend. How many times did I need to be reminded? "The book is dead. The CD-ROM never lived. You can get everything you need on a phone. And then some. We need to think about this…" I argued that the book wasn't dead: it just needed to evolve. "A generation of people will always prefer a book," I said. "Think about that. They said vinyl was dead. Look at it now. Retro is cool, and one day books will be cool and people will sneer at apps. And what's a blog but a load of egocentric insights peppered with poor jokes, bad punctuation and poorly framed selfies with some landscape in the out-of-focus background? The only people who read them are the people who write them. I mean, are you interested in what your neighbour did last week in Morocco?" Some people nodded at this last point, but were careful to lace their nods with a shot of negativity. And then the meeting broke up and Cora refused to talk to me for a couple of hours.

I crossed out words, sentences, paragraphs and then realized I didn't know where to stop, so I tossed the notebook across the room and picked up my phone. I had no texts, no messages and the battery was low. I plugged it in, poured another glass of wine and sent a text to Daniel. "Thanks for coming. You're a good mate. Hope you got back OK." Then, in one of those moments that dare you, I thumbed one to Cora. It said: "I meant it when I said I was sorry. Sorry about being more than a fool. I wish you were here. It's freezing. I miss you. M x." I thumbed the text, but I didn't send it. I dropped the phone on the floor and let it charge.

Lassitude is a cruel thing. It holds hands with sadness and laughs at your impotence. It has no shame, and doesn't care if the most you can do is lie in a pit of imagined exhaustion. I can gorge on the stuff, have it drip from my lips and stain my tie. Sometimes for an hour, sometimes for a week, sometimes for a month, but the cruelty is bitter. It leaves scars. If you'd been here, I'd have lifted my shirt and shown you the scar that runs from the back of my neck to my waist, parallel to my spine. And if you'd wanted, I'd have shown you another – the one on the back of my left eye. But maybe not.

I dozed for half an hour and woke to the sound of a ping. I picked up my phone. I expected to see a reply from Daniel. What I got was a reply from Cora. I'd sent her the text without knowing I'd sent it. Cold and nervous, I poured myself half a glass of wine before checking her reply. It read: "Sorry to hear you're freezing. Cold here too. Maybe we got off on the wrong foot. Got a gin here so whatever. C x." I looked at my watch. It was half-past three. I left the phone on the couch and went to bed.

EXCUSES

Cora. I lusted after her, loved her, loved spending silent hours with her, loved reading with her and listening to music and dripping wine onto her stomach. She had a small, round stomach, like a half-risen loaf. Sometimes I would rest my ear against it and listen to it. So when she told me she wanted a break, that she didn't like the feeling of being "cooped up" and wasn't ready to commit to anything, I laughed. Probably not the best laugh I'd ever given her, or the best thing I ever did, but I couldn't stop myself. And when I said I thought it was men who were afraid to commit, she said it was best not to believe everything I read. And when I asked her if she thought we still had a chance to make it work, she said: "If we have to work to make it work, then it's not working." I don't like nonsense dressed up as wisdom or aphorism, and I told her so, and by the end of the week, our relationship had sunk like a soufflé. And all this under the noses of our colleagues at Tread Lightly, people who were busy enough with their work and travels, but not busy enough to ignore the atmosphere that bubbled between us. I suppose that if she'd said she'd wanted a break because she didn't like me stealing toothpaste from high-street chemists, I'd have understood. But she never said that, because she didn't know. I never told her. So when I met Daniel for a drink and he asked me what had happened, I was telling the truth when I said I didn't know.

"I think she wants some space, but she hasn't told me why."

"Give her some time."

"Yeah, right. Time. I don't like time."

"You don't like time? What sort of idea is that?"

"My sort of idea."

It's true. I don't like time. I don't like the way it hangs around on corners and sneaks up on you. I don't like the way it never waits for you. It's pushy, endless and limitless, and that makes it arrogant. And I don't like it because Cora used to say she had time on her side, like it was someone she met at a party. And then she said I shouldn't be sad because it was over, but smile because it had happened. When she said that I cringed. It took me weeks to get the rhythm of those words out of my head. They stayed in there, banging around like a bat in a box. And cringing is against my nature. I don't like nature either, but that's another story.

NATURE

A few months before I left for Italy, I caught a train, took some of my memories for a walk in the country and had a long talk with them. I sat in the corner of a field in Kent and sneezed. I like Kent. I like the shadows in the air, the ghosts of the hop-pickers and the phantom gypsies who wait at crossroads with their bows and bags. And I like to imagine the pilgrims as they walked to Canterbury, singing and laughing and telling their stories in the evening inns – the bad meat and mushrooms and oats soaked in brine, and the wooden cups of brew. I watched some cows and wondered what they were doing. Why did they stand in a line, and why did they lie down together in those patches of dirt? I saw some birds, listened to them singing and thought that one day I would buy a book and find out about their songs, their nesting habits and how when they flew down chimneys they made people run from their homes in fear.

Cora and I used to take mini-breaks to places like Bourton-on-the-Water and Pontrhydfendigaid and Chagford, and as I sat in the Kentish field and twirled a piece of straw around my fingers, I wondered if my heart had crawled from me. The meadows and woods and valleys were too quiet, and the clouds in the sky were still.

I told my memories that if they didn't stop hassling me, I would leave them. My memories didn't believe me. They laughed at me. They had a deep laugh, like they had spent too long living in a damp trench without a coat. My memories and I took a deep breath, looked away from the view and, after we'd batted insults backwards and forwards, we made an agreement. If they agreed to stop bothering me at odd times, I wouldn't add any new bad ones to their tally. Easy to say, difficult to promise.

POSITANO

Can inanimate things think? Do they have feelings? Do they know when you eat a green salad or go to bed? Can they wait half an hour and force your dreams into a small box? Can inanimate things sit in a walnut bureau and purr? Do they wish for a parcel of tissue and an envelope to keep them warm? Do they sleep, wake up at half-past four and stare at the ceiling, go back to sleep and wonder through the rest of the boxed dreams? Do they have their own syntax?

So many questions. More questions. Can you fall in love with an inanimate thing? Can an inanimate thing fall in love with you? Is possession half love? Is love why rich people have paintings stolen to order and keep them in vaults? Is theft love's motivation? Is love an excuse for cruelty? Is love found or learnt? I like questions, especially when they can't be answered.

After reading Cora's text, I slept for an hour and woke around five. I could hear things scratching – a bird on the window sill – a spider in the wall – a dozen ants carrying crumbs of bread to a hole in the ceiling – a couple of dogs arguing about clouds. I turned and lay on my right side, tucked my hand under the pillow, pulled the sheet over my face, closed my eyes and listened. The scratching had stopped. I fell asleep and didn't remember my dreams.

When I woke again, it was half-past ten. The sun was lancing through a crack in the shutters, cutting lines across the ceiling and down the wall above the bedhead. I lay still for a few minutes, then got out of bed and padded to the kitchen. I made some tea and stood at the window and watched two men saunter across the beach. They were wearing hats and carrying buckets, and when they reached a pile of rocks, they stopped and one of them pointed at the sky. I sipped the tea, ate a banana and then went to the bathroom. I showered quickly and, while I was dressing, I booted my laptop and checked my emails. Nothing important dropped into the inbox, so I grabbed my coat, pouched my notebook and a fist of self-awareness and went to work.

Self-awareness begins when you realize – and accept – that you're not as clever as you think you are. It's a tough call, but simple enough, and once you make it, you're almost home. You see yourself, you see your eyes and your skin and your mouth, and you peer inside your brain, you listen to the things you say, recall the things you've done, and then you're free to work your way up. The thought is simple, the road is paved, but the rest is difficult. I was thinking this on the bus to Positano. I said "Fool…" to myself. I'd replied to Cora's text.

Positano was closed. It wasn't closed when John Steinbeck visited and described it as a dream place – and he wasn't wrong. He was a good writer and owned a faithful dog. The locked church, the shuttered shops, the boarded-up guest houses, the cafés and restaurants with chairs on tables and pots of paint on the floor, the litter blowing down the empty streets, the cats curled tight on doorsteps – all gave the impression of a place pulled from a sleeper's tossings. I sat on a step and felt my phone in my pocket. I put a hand in my other pocket and pulled out my notebook and wrote...

But this is the joy of travelling in the very out-of-season season, for as you walk the deserted streets, the place is in your pocket. You could even say it is your pocket, and as you weave your way through the beached fishing boats on the sand, you can hardly imagine that in August this place will be thronged with thousands of people, and a relaxed stroll would be impossible.

I took a path from the main strand and walked under spreading pine trees, past a tower to a beach where the emptiness was heightened by broody cliffs, piles of litter and clots of smoke from an unattended fire. A dog snoozed on a pile of sticks, and the sea sucked at grey sand. I strolled in the old way, feet scuffing, head down, looking for washed-up stuff, and for a while was happy with my own company – maybe more than happy.

I found flakes of terracotta in the sand. Some were plain, others winked with colour: blue mainly, some white and pink. I collected a few, rubbed them between my fingers and thumb, licked them, tried them between my teeth and put them in my pocket. The dog watched me, and when I came to a place where the beach faded into rocks, I found a place to sit and watch the waves. They were small and perfect – kittens of water. I took my phone out of my pocket and read the text I'd sent Cora. I decided that we're all trapped in an hour, but we make its moments. "Gin sounds good. Like gin tho like whisky better.

Gin gives me headache in morning. I like you too. Don't like wrong feet either. x"

I hadn't had a reply. It didn't matter. I was here and she was there, and it was only miles between us. I sat on the rocks, and the dog watched me and I watched the waves. I wasn't bothered. I could turn my mouth inside out, die, and no one would know. The gulls could take my eyes and make something useful out of them.

I often think about my dying. I see cancer killing me as I lie in a caravan above a beach in the west of Ireland, but sometimes I'm shot by accident in a rabbit field. Embrace fate. This is my ideal. Embrace it, hold it tight – and if it tries to wriggle, pat its head. Make life the victory. Montaigne wrote: "All the wisdom and argument in the world eventually comes down to one conclusion, which is to teach us not to be afraid of dying…" and he was right. I want peace and I want rest, and I want the dark. I look forward to the day when I won't be chased by thorns and shards, and the box I can't feel rolls towards the flames. And I look forward to silence – the floating of clouds over someone else's memories, and the plaster cast of another's thoughts. It's easy, but then so is whatever you choose to be difficult.

FOOD

I had dinner in Amalfi, in an empty place with a view of the street and the *passeggiata*. As the men and women strolled and children skipped around them, the sun dropped into a bank of clouds that turned pink and gold along their edges. The lights of a freighter twinkled, and a high plane lay its contrail across the horizon. I took a deep breath and a pen, and wrote some gentle burble.

Sometimes, eating alone in an empty restaurant can be a dispiriting experience. The thought you could be sitting with friends, surrounded by companionable strangers, tucking into good food, listening to stimulating conversation, the wine flowing, blah blah blah... But then sometimes all you want is to be alone with the gentle burble of the local radio, the evening lights flickering in the streets, the tidy waitress, the guttering candles...

I ordered a jug of white wine and a bowl of spaghetti with a salad on the side, and as I twirled the pasta and listened to the cook laugh at a television, I thought about food in Britain.

Food in Britain isn't something I think much about, but when I do I feel the choler rise, for my thought is this: food in Britain is fetishized. If pornography is masturbatory and eroticism is celebratory, then British food is porn and Italian, Spanish, French and the rest are erotic. So I'm stretching the metaphor, but the more I listen to British chefs talk about "fresh" and "local" and "seasonal" (as if we need reminding) the more I want to take them outside. So we came to good food late and we need to be told what to do and how to do it, but it's the constancy of the telling and the self-satisfaction of the tellers. Of course an orange fresh from the tree is tastier than an orange picked last month, transported a thousand miles, ethylene-ripened in a warehouse outside Slough, dropped into a plastic net and sold in a supermarket, but don't remind me. And I know the words "farm-fresh" are a euphemism, and I know scrambled eggs continue to cook after you've removed them from the heat. And I know something about wine. And when I see a tomato with a stalk I don't need to be told that it was grown on a vine. So I'm not expressing myself well – I lose the ability to do anything well when I'm angry – but all I want is a warm plate and something that tastes. And I don't need to be reminded what it is I ordered. And I don't want to be interrupted ten minutes in to be asked if I'm enjoying my meal. If I'm not, I'll tell you. It's simple. As simple as an unusual feeling of superiority that had crept up on me.

I suppose it was related to the feeling of pride I'd felt that morning – its brother or maybe its cousin? What was the phrase? "All day long the superior man is creatively active"? Or is the superior man simply spending his days hoarding jewels in a heavy chest? And looking down his nose at people simply because they've got a moral compass?

I didn't like the feeling of feeling superior. There seemed no point to it, and it felt like I'd been invaded by dust, so I caught the waitress's eye and ordered another glass of wine. When she came back, she asked me if I'd had a good day. I told her I'd been to Positano, and she winced. "Positano is no good," she said, and when I told her it was closed, she laughed and patted the table. She had perfect, beautiful nails. I wanted to cover them.

It was a slow evening, the sort of evening that turns its back on the day and refuses to believe in the coming night. A quiet one, a grave of a few hours – a stranger's grave, visited by a few people for a few years, then forgotten and left to itself. I laid some flowers, finished the wine, stood up and went to the door. I joined the *passeggiata* in the way that only an Englishman can, left it at the top of the promenade and climbed the steps to the path that led through the old houses to Atrani.

THE OLD PATH

Atrani could be Amalfi's Piraeus (actually it couldn't be, so do something about this), and the best way to reach it from the main town is to take a path that climbs away from the coast road, up flights of old steps, under ancient arches and past shuttered doors and windows. Washing hangs, the smell of cooking wafts in the air, glasses clink. Voices shout, women cry, men howl. On a cold winter night, there is no better way to warm frozen bones (I can think of a better way), and when you reach the top, the views across the bay are…

However you do it, and whatever the books and blogs say about leisurely strolls into Mediterranean bliss, the walk from Amalfi to Atrani is a slog. The steps from the main road are worn and many, and when they turn and climb past the first houses they steepen and disappear into echoes and damp. But I'd had enough wine to kick me, and by the time I reached the path that hugs the cliff I was feeling good enough to shout. So I leant on the wall and yelled the first word that came to my mind. I didn't think – I just let it come. And as her name disappeared into the night, I thought of my love and how our ruins were only that. Their walls had poured into a valley, and roof tiles were smashed across the rocks. Clouds were building, and everything was cut by shadows.

There was a dark house below me, and a neatly tilled terrace of earth – a lemon tree, a piece of corrugated iron banging against a whitewashed wall, a ladder and a dog. Further down, the corniche and a tunnel, and the canvassed lights of a restaurant. The smell of cooking fish drifted towards me, the sound of tinkling glass and laughing couples. Cars passed, and scooters, and a man on a bicycle. The chug of a fishing boat carried across the sea, and the lights of Salerno twinkled along the horizon. I felt a glittering, something to do with the wine, food, view and a memory. I heard a shout, the call of a woman to her lover, an echo of my own shout, the same feeling lost in a bled sky. I watched the moon for a while, then walked on, down the path, around the slow dark bends and up the last few steps to my door. I stood to get my breath back, heard a song in my head, tried to grab its chorus, let it go, let it come back, found the key, stuck it in the lock, turned, heard the chorus again, shot it, pushed, pushed harder, let the door swing and let myself in.

I walked through to the kitchen, poured a glass of wine and sat by the window. I felt myself slide into loss. A foolish thing to do, but something I'd done before, and as I slid I thought of England, grey skies and home.

My home was a flat in Bermondsey, four rooms with a view of a pub and a row of shops, and when I went to bed I'd spend half an hour listening to wailing and the shouts of edged lives. Home was a place that wrung its hands against the door, left its spit in the letterbox and stalked to the pub. Dull pavements, red buses, blue lights from shops that never closed. Lost? Found? I sipped the wine. A moment later the phone rang. I didn't look at the screen. I answered. Cora took a breath and said: "So what did you do today?"

We were good at starting a conversation as if we were in the middle of one.

"I went to Positano."

"How was it?"

"Empty."

"Good copy?"

"I don't know. I hope so. That's for you to say."

"You need to know, Matt."

"I'd rather you told me."

"OK. It's good copy. Brilliant copy."

"I know. I'm a genius."

"No you're not. You're a hack."

"So I am. I'm a hack in a dying industry."

"You don't have to be, Matt. You choose your gallery."

"My gallery?"

"Yes, Matt. Your gallery."

We talked like this for a few more minutes, batting the other's questions with nothings until we stopped and listened to the other's silence.

"You know," I said, "I meant what I said. So I might have been drunk, but that doesn't mean I didn't know what I was saying."

"And what did you say?"

"I said I was sorry. And I said I wished you were here."

"And why the hell would you want me there? Not getting any joy with the locals?"

"I like…" I said. "I like sitting next to you."

"That sounds weird."

"Why?"

"It sounds like you're imagining us in church or something."

"Well…"

"Yes?"

"It occurred to me a few days ago. We're good at sitting next to each other. You know, not saying anything. Just being comfortable. I like being comfortable."

"I know."

"And what does that mean?"

"You know exactly what it means. You need to start acknowledging some truths about yourself, Matt."

"Oh, I've started doing that already."

"Of course you have."

"Really…"

"Go on then. Name one. Name one truth…"

"I don't know…"

She laughed.

"Why the laugh?"

"Because… because you're a challenge."

"You make me sound like a jigsaw."

"No, Matt. You're simpler than that."

"Thanks."

"You're welcome."

Another silence. I let it hang, listened to its beat, imagined her sitting in her flat with a glass of gin on the table, papers on the floor, street lamps cutting the blinds and lighting the ceiling. I wondered what she was wearing. I used to ask her what she was wearing and she used to tell me. I left it.

"Look," I said.

"What?"

"Let's talk when I get back."

"About what?"

"You know."

"No, I don't. Tell me."

"Us, I suppose…"

"Us?"

"Yes."

Another silence. I was tired. I poured some more wine. I heard her pour another gin. I heard the clink of ice against glass.

"We could talk now," she said.

"I'm tired," I said.

"Or drunk?"

"Both," I said.

"I thought so."

"You got a problem with that?"

"I don't have problems," she said. "Only solutions."

And so it went for another five minutes, the two of us sniping and repeating, two dogs chasing our tails until we were exhausted, and she said "I'll text" and I said "I'll look out for it", and she hung up.

I went and stood on the terrace, looked down at the town, watched the road for a few minutes, listened to voices from the black beach, and then I went to sit in the living room. I let my need for Cora breed, and then I let this need bleed and fester. My feelings started to grow and twist and turn into something like power. I didn't turn the light on – and then, as the night settled around me and the old man in the apartment next door hacked his way to sleep, I felt a nostalgic comfort overtake the feeling of power, sideswipe it and force it off the road. So I was confused, but I wasn't complicated. I was too simple. I like the dark, and so does Cora, and for a moment I was tempted to call her back and ask if she remembered a particular night in my flat, but I stopped myself. Some memories are best left to die.

THE DREAM OF MY COUSIN

I went to bed and thought about the trouble with love and what happens when it's overtaken by pride or fear or guilt. It moulds itself to circumstance, melts into chairs and beds, switches sides. You have an argument and wonder if you've done the right thing. What used to be so sweet becomes salty. Perfect skin suddenly looks like the skin of a bean. Love could be death. Everything you thought was ideal is made of paper.

Death, I thought, and paper. I lay on my side. The man next door snuffled. I heard footsteps in the alley outside, and voices. I couldn't hear what they were saying. They talked for five minutes and then stopped. I turned and lay on my other side and closed my eyes. I slipped away and, once I was gone, I had a dream. In this dream, I had a distant cousin. We didn't know each other well, and one day, when we were in our twenties, we met for the first time in years. The moment I saw her, I fell in love with her. She had an oval face, shoulder-length wavy brown hair and a large mouth. The most amazing thing about her was her confidence. It was as though she knew everything and had been everywhere. She hadn't, but that's how it seemed to me. She wore her confidence lightly. I felt small next to her, and awed, and in my dream I started to dream about her. And in the dream I had in the dream I had another dream, and so it went, in the manner of mirrors facing each other.

For a month or two, I meet my dream cousin for coffee or a drink. There were always happy people around. She attracted them. One day, someone suggested to me that she and I should get married. I said I wasn't sure. "We're cousins," I said. "Distant," said the person.

"Your great-great-great-grandmother is her great-great-great-grandmother; that makes you fourth cousins."

"True," I said, so the next day I asked her if she would marry me.

"Of course," she said.

I was overwhelmed and said: "I love you so much."

"I like you now," she said, "but I'm going to learn to love you."

Over the next few months, we made arrangements for the wedding, and when we met (usually at outdoor gatherings of our extended family or in gazebos), we circled around each other in a friendly way, but never displayed affection in a big way. We'd decided to keep our relationship secret until the day of the wedding, so when I touched her arm or stroked her hair, people simply thought I was being friendly. And when she laughed at my stupid jokes, people simply thought she was being kind.

Remember – this is a dream, but the wedding happened like this: we invited the celebrant to one of our family gatherings and introduced her as one of my friends. Two of our other cousins were in on the plan and, at a prearranged signal, they asked people to stand in two rows facing each other. Our family were always ready for a surprise and happy to oblige a whim, so they did as they were told. Then the celebrant took her place at the far end of the two rows, and my fourth cousin and I walked towards her. As we walked, the penny dropped, and people said

"I think they're getting married…" and then they said "They are getting married…" and people smiled, and some started to cry and others hugged.

I don't remember the ceremony itself, but I do remember afterwards as we walked back past the rows of people, and they were applauding and throwing their hats in the air and saying things like "This calls for a drink!" Wine was bought, and trays of food, and then we were in a beautiful garden, and I looked at my cousin and was overwhelmed with love for her. In my dream I could feel this love pressing down on my chest, and when I told her how much I loved her, she said: "I like you. And I'm going to learn to love you."

The next thing I knew, we were leaving the garden and travelling to our honeymoon, and then she had to go back to work. She worked for the Canadian Railways, and drove a train from Winnipeg to Vancouver. She said I could come with her, but only if I made her some sandwiches. So that's what I did. And when we stopped at a bend in a river with a view of the Rockies, she climbed down from her cab and walked back to where I was sitting in a carriage, and I stepped out and gave her the sandwiches. She looked at them and said: "Would you like to ride with me?"

"Yes," I said, and we walked back to the cab, and I sat next to her and she ate the sandwiches. When she'd finished them, she turned to me and said "I've learnt to love you", and then she started the train and drove it towards the mountains. And as the train started to climb, it started to make a rattling sound over the rails. The dream began to fade, and I woke up. I was lying on my back. The rattling sound didn't fade. Someone was trying to open the apartment door.

THE WATER TANK

I swung my legs out of bed and stood up. Whoever was outside knocked on the door, rattled the knob and called my name. "Signor Baxter?" It was a woman's voice. I recognized it from somewhere. "Please open the door."

"Yes…" I called. "I'm coming."

"Thank you," said the woman.

"Give me a moment."

"Of course."

"A minute…"

"We are waiting."

I had slept in my clothes, so all I had to do was rub my eyes and my head, and do up my shirt buttons. I noticed a stain on my sleeve. I think it was a wine stain. Red wine. I couldn't remember. It didn't matter.

I wasn't wearing shoes, but that didn't matter either. I took a deep breath, took the five steps from the bedroom to the hallway, turned the key in the lock and opened the door. Arabella, the owner of the flat, was standing on the step. A man was standing behind her. "I'm disturbing you," she said, "but you have a leak."

I reached out and grabbed the door frame. I said "I'm sorry?" – but the words sounded wrong.

"Here." She pointed around the corner. On the roof above the apartment, a cylindrical water tank was dribbling water into the gutter. She stepped to one side. "This is Marco. He will fix it." Marco nodded and held up a canvas bag. "He'll need to turn your water off for an hour, so can we come inside?"

Her words echoed in my head. I let them flip around in there for a few seconds, and then I said "Of course", stepped back and let them inside.

They were in the flat for ten minutes. They looked for stop-cocks and did stuff in the kitchen, and then Marco went to fetch a ladder. When he was gone, Arabella asked me if I was enjoying my stay, and when I said I was, she put her hand on my arm and said: "Are you well? You look so pale."

"I haven't been sleeping."

"I don't think it's too noisy here," she said.

"No," I said. "It's not that. I never sleep very well."

"I'm sorry. Maybe you need to see a doctor. My brother is a doctor."

"It's OK. Thank you – but I don't need a doctor."

Marco came back with a ladder, propped it against the out-side wall and started doing something with a pair of spanners.

"Well," said Arabella, "I have to go back to work. Will you be here for an hour? I think Marco will need to test the water when he's finished on the roof."

"I'll be here."

"Good." She put her hand on my arm again. "I hope you get some good sleep tonight."

"So do I," I said.

PAPER MILLS

I walk every day. Sometimes it's a stroll to the shops, occasionally it's an amble along the South Bank, a few times it's been a hike across a northern moor or along a Cornish coast path. It's the only exercise that won't kill you. It doesn't put any strain on your knees, there's no resistance and you don't have to run. Someone said you should only run for two reasons: if you're trying to catch a bus or if you're attempting to escape from a predator. Some people can be too wise for their own good, and other people can be stupid. Usually, the people who think they're wise are stupid, while the stupid are just stupid. It's the gauche who show the most wisdom, and the apparently intelligent who have no idea. Or not. It depends on my mood and theirs, and the sort of exercise they take.

After Marco had finished on the roof, tested the water and told me I was staying in the best apartment in Atrani, I had a shave, chose a long raincoat instead of my leather jacket and took a walk to the ruined paper mills in the gorge behind Amalfi.

Paper-making was one of the industries that helped Amalfi become a powerful maritime republic, and the simple techniques – combining cotton and pure mountain water – are still practised in the town. But it's further up the valley that the full extent of the ancient industry's remains can be seen.

For here, in the shadow of rocky crags and wooded outcrops, the crumbling ruins of half a dozen mills dominate the lonely landscape...

I walked through the town and took a path that led away from the houses, climbing past open doors, the smell of simmering tomato sauce, the burble of television football and the sound of someone working in the lemon orchards – a hoe sorting through the earth, stones and gravel – the scents of metal and acid, the bark of a distant dog. Here and there, the path turned to steep steps, and when the last of the houses were behind me, the path became a stony track.

Someone – a philosopher, probably – wrote: "It is solved by walking." He never said what the "it" was, but there's no doubt he was wrong. I would say whatever the "it" is is complicated by walking, and troubles are concentrated by the act of putting one foot in front of the other. For once you've got past the views, smells, exercise, sounds, occasional meetings with strangers, what are you left with? You're left with your thoughts, and if they're as nagging as mine, you're in trouble. For my thoughts hounded me, and as I stumbled towards the first of the ruined mills, I clipped my head on a low-hanging branch. As the pain spread and a bruise swelled and grew, I was reminded of a time when Cora and I took a holiday in Prague, and I knocked myself out on the poorly designed handrail of a tram. And as I thought about Prague and its bad-tempered trams, my mind ran to something she had said to me in our dark hotel room in that old city. "You'll always be a hack – a good hack, mind – but a hack all the same." I'd told her I was going to publish my novel. "Forget it," she said. "You're forty-five. If you were going to publish a novel, you'd have done it by now."

"But I want to be a writer," I said. "A real writer."

"You can't *want* to be a writer," she said. "You have to *be* one."

"And who are you quoting now?"

"I've no idea."

I couldn't argue with that, and as we lay in the cold bed and my head throbbed with pain, a church bell chimed eleven. I opened my mouth to say something about the bell being the first music we'd heard since arriving in the city, but I didn't want to be trite. Cora sat up, looked at my bruise and said: "Maybe you should see a doctor about that."

"It'll be OK."

"My brave boy," she said.

"That's me," I said, and I felt her hand take mine and squeeze it. I squeezed back, but in that moment I knew we were doomed. There was an unsaid resignation about the way we talked to each other, made love, shared a table, walked into a museum, walked around a museum, walked out of a museum, found a bar, sat to drink beer: everything we did together was freighted with pain and inevitability. Maybe we stayed together because we loved shadow and gloom. Maybe we both wanted a permanent argument in our lives. It sounds ridiculous, but take a look around next time you're shopping or on a train or on holiday, and wonder.

Back in the hills above Amalfi, I rubbed my bruise and climbed on, and when I reached an outcrop of rock, I turned and stared back at the paper mill. Its ruined walls and blank windows stood above a tumbling stream and scrubby hillsides. Signs warned people to keep out. I was wondering what to do – walk on for another mile or turn around and go back – when a pair of hikers appeared below me, walking at a clip, their sticks clicking on the rocks and their coats rustling against the cold – a man and a woman. They stopped by a gatepost, slipped rucksacks off their backs and sat on a log. The woman took a flask from her sack and poured two cups of something hot, and the man pulled a copy of the *Tread Lightly Guide to Italy* out of his pocket, turned to a marked page and started to read aloud.

"Paper-making was one of the industries that helped Amalfi become a powerful maritime republic, and the simple techniques – combining cotton and pure mountain water – are still practised in the town. But it's further up the valley that the full extent of the ancient industry can be seen. For here, in the shadow of rocky crags and wooded outcrops, the crumbling ruins of half a dozen mills dominate the lonely landscape…"

"Interesting," said the woman.

"Isn't it?" said the man. "Who'd have imagined that these mills used to produce the finest paper in the world?"

"Not me," said the woman, and she passed the man his drink. He smiled, planted a kiss on her cheek and whispered something in her ear. I stood up quietly and walked on, across the outcrop and up to a little stone bridge that carried the path over the stream. I stood there for ten minutes and watched the water for ten minutes, and then I realized that I had nothing else to say and nothing else to think about the old paper mills, and nothing to write in my notebook, so I turned and headed back into town. And as I walked, I thought about lemons and work and Cora, and I thought that sometimes the edge of the world is simply the road we walk from one gift to the next.

DINNER IN AMALFI

I ate in the quiet restaurant by the town square, the table with a
street view, a jug of local wine and the bored waitress. I ordered
lasagne, drank half a glass of the wine and took out my phone.
Cora had texted: "Where's my text?" I texted back: "Sorry. I've
been walking. And working. You know how it is." She pinged
back five minutes later. "No, I don't. How is it?" I replied with
"I'm eating. I'll call later." She replied with "Stuff your face, fat
boy." I thought about this, turned the phone over, opened my
notebook and wrote some lines about the day.

*The paper mills have gone, their broached and tumbled walls
returning to the gorges that created them, and the mountain
streams that fed the industry run clear again. But if, on a bright
winter afternoon, you have the luck to be alone among the
ruins, it's easy to imagine the noise and bustle of an industry
that dominated this area and provided work for generations
of Amalfians... (Amalfians? Is that what they are called?) And
if you're lucky enough to be with someone close, someone
you love, you can be sure that the experience will be more
than simple, and something that stays with you for as long
as you live. (Want to get any more personal here? Why don't
you tell everyone?)*

My food arrived, and I put the notebook in my pocket and poured another glass of wine.

The waitress turned a television on and watched with the sound off for a couple of minutes. Then she went and stood by the door and said: "You were here before."

"I was."

"You're German?"

"No."

"Then you're English."

"Yes," I said. "How did you guess?"

"Only the English eat so early – or drink so fast. Like the Germans…"

"I was hungry."

"You can eat at any time of day," she said. "It means nothing to me."

"Thank you," I said. "Would you like a drink?"

"You're buying me one?"

"Of course."

She looked towards the kitchen. I heard the chef. He was talking on the phone. "OK," she said. "Thank you," and she went to a bar, took a bottle of Coke from the fridge, poured it into a glass and raised it to me.

"Cheers," I said.

"*Salute*," she said, and she turned to look towards the street.

She had dark hair, a blitz of spots on her forehead and footballer's legs. Her uniform was black and buttoned to her neck, and the little white apron she wore covered a round belly. She was halfway through her drink when the door opened and a little boy ran in. "Mamma!" he cried, and ran to her. She bent down and hugged him, ran her fingers through his hair and asked him what he'd been doing. "*Stavo giocando,*" he said, and he told her about a dog he and his friends had found on the beach.

If Cora and I had had a son, I supposed he could have been this boy's age now. Five? Six? I wasn't sure, but once I started to go down this road, and the trees beside the road began to lean towards me, I began to feel sad. The wine didn't help, so I drank some more.

My sadness was like a spot of oil dropped into a harbour's water, spreading and colouring and drawing notice. I'd never seen colours like them, had never thought about kids before. Until that moment they had been an irritation, a reason for strangers' self-satisfaction, the focus of attention that people who used to be friends imposed on the order of our lives. Noisy, dirty, demanding, smelly, wet and incomprehensible, but I still felt a sort of longing – at least I think that's what it was – rising like a kite over my dry heart. I could have tugged the string, turned it away from the wind and let it fall, but the more I thought so, the more I enjoyed the feeling, the welling and the catching behind my eyes. For what is it like to know that someone walks the earth who walks because of you? What is it like to know you'll always get at least one birthday card? What is it like to have someone phone you for no other reason than you're you? What is it like to love someone unconditionally and have them love back in the same way? What is it like to give someone two thousand pounds because they tell you they need a car? And why had I never thought about children before? Was it because my next birthday was a big one? Would I start to buy magazines about motorbikes? Would I start to weep for no reason? Why did the waitress's son smile at me? Why did I smile back? And what is it like to have to get up in the middle of the night even though you're tired?

I caught the waitress's eye and asked for a coffee. I looked at my phone. Nothing. She came back with the coffee, put it on the table and picked up my plate.

"Was it good?"

"Yes. Thank you. And thank the chef."

"I will." She waited for a moment, and her free hand rested on the tablecloth. "Anything else with your coffee?"

"No thanks."

"It would be on the house…"

"That's kind of you," I said, "but I think I've had enough."

"OK," she said, and she shrugged and turned and headed towards the kitchen. I watched her go and then picked up my coffee and drank. I stayed in the restaurant for ten more minutes, then dropped some cash on the table and pushed my way into the night.

A DRINK IN AMALFI

I found a lit bar where a crowd was watching football and I could drink in a corner. I ordered whisky, took a sip, let it hit the back of my throat and looked up at the television.

The team in blue scored. The bar erupted. A kid came from behind the bar to look at the replay of the goal. His father picked him up so he could get a better view, and they hugged each other when the ball went into the net and the footballers danced to the crowd and yelled their joy. The whisky was a brand I hadn't heard of, but it was good.

Cora and I never talked about having kids, but we never gave each other the chance to talk about a lot of things. We didn't talk about why she read a newspaper and I never did – we didn't talk about the pros and cons of zoos – and we didn't talk about why I'd never used a hot tub, though I did tell her that if she'd seen the hair and dead skin that accumulates in a hot-tub filter she'd never use one either. I never told her that I stole something every couple of months, and she never told me… what did she never tell me about herself? There must have been secrets in her life. She must have done things she was ashamed of, things she wanted to forget, things she was afraid might fly. But our relationship was born of lust, cooked in need and left to cool in a knackered kitchen, and when we got round to talking about anything serious, it was always about how we were going to repair ruins. I suppose we got off on the wrong foot and stayed on the wrong foot all the way, and there was always a stone in the shoe. I knew it and she knew it. We just didn't know how to take the shoe off.

The team in blue scored again. I pulled out my phone and pinged: "Finished eating. Drinking now. Talk later?"

"Give me an hour or two," came back a moment later. "I've got to get rid of Sam."

Sam? What?

I tapped "Who the hell is Sam?"

"Wouldn't you like to know?"

"Yes."

No reply.

"Hello?"

Nothing.

So now, joining my thoughts about kids and blame and trouble and whisky, came thoughts about someone called Sam – his shoes off, his feet up on Cora's occasional table, a glass of Soave in one hand and her breast cupped in the other, a satisfied smile on his pasty face, a glow in her eyes. Him putting the glass on the table and using a damp finger to twirl a curl of her hair, her giggling something into his ear – him laughing, her blushing – him whispering something about how the evening couldn't be more perfect, her saying it could be improved. Him suggesting they watch a movie or cook some eggs or share a shower or discuss the issues that have caused such distress in the Levant – her suggesting they do all four at the same time. Him laughing and showing his dazzling teeth – her tweaking the end of his nose like he was a cute bear with soft paws and a pizza on order.

And as my thoughts swilled together and I drank a third whisky, the second unrecognized feeling of the evening popped into my mind – or was it the third – or maybe the fourth? Whatever. Jealousy. At least that's what I think it was. A flushing in my body – my heart pumping blood faster than usual – the hairs on my skin standing up. Sometimes I like to trot out a personal cliché – and I've always told myself I wasn't the jealous type. Sometimes I like to eat crisps. And sometimes I like to drink more whisky before imagining I have a gun in my hand and a cross of bullets on my chest.

DRUNK IN ATRANI

I read somewhere that there's no such thing as an addictive personality. I've also known people who like to think they're doctors because they can use a search engine and know how to spell haematologist or because they've worked as a hospital porter or because they love arguing with authority figures. My father was a consultant cardiologist, and he used to tell the story of the patient who argued with his diagnosis of valvular disease because the volunteer who pushed the library trolley around the wards told her that all she had was a cold. And the angriest people are the people who claim they're lovers. And the people who say there's no such thing as an addictive personality are wrong. And the most beautiful picture in the world is not in a gallery. And Ernest Moeran wrote the greatest English symphony. And most people don't understand why the sommelier offers them a taste of wine before pouring the bottle. And I've never met a Christian.

It took me an hour to get home. I had to climb half the steps to Atrani on my hands and knees, and when I got to the top and the path with the view of the sea, I leant over the wall and puked. I remember doing the raging thing drunk people do, slashing at the air, grabbing the corners of my coat and spinning around, pointing at the lights of Salerno and the stars, feeling them in their cursed orbits and asking them what the hell they thought they were doing. I felt my arms go limp and I felt myself stop, and then I stared at the sky in wonder. So it was drunk wonder, but it was wonder – true wonder, the wonder of a child who sees the sea for the first time. Some of the light I could see was millions of years old. I know people who say that when you look at a star you're looking back in time, but you're not. You're simply looking at something old. I have a friend called Rupert who told me that when you burn something, the flame you see is stored sunlight released. I say I have a friend, but he died when the car he was travelling in crashed into the back of a petrol tanker, so I don't have him any more. But I have my memories of him and his wisdom – and when I think of the times he used to ring me up and ask if I wanted to go fishing with him, I fill with sadness. For I never went fishing with Rupert, never took a train with him to Ramsgate, climbed into an open boat with a crusty old man in a hat and sailed out to look for whiting. Fishing – I thought – is dangerous, and then I felt my neck fail and I didn't think about fishing any more. I stumbled backwards, hit my back against a wall and slipped to the ground. I saw myself as the ground, and then I saw myself as a brick, and then I was a building, and then my head was a leaking roof. Someone came and built scaffolding around me, and then they took it away because no one had paid the bill. I looked for the scaffolder, but he had gone. I was alone. I tried to stand up. I failed. I crawled for five minutes, maybe ten, and then I came to the steps by my apartment. They were wet. I slipped and I swore. An orange light was shining. It took me five minutes to get the key in my door, and two more minutes to crawl down the hallway to the living room. I found the sofa, crawled onto it and fell asleep.

I woke up two hours later. I was freezing. I touched my nose. It was running. I heard someone screaming, birds singing, dogs barking, cats purring and more dogs barking. I pulled myself to the bedroom, dropped my coat on the floor, climbed into bed, buried myself in the blankets and fell asleep again. I dreamt I was trying to play tennis in fog. I couldn't see my opponent and only saw the ball when it was inches away, and I lost every game. I woke again as the sun was rising. I fell out of bed, rolled to the kitchen and drank a glass of water. I went to the toilet and went back to the bedroom. My head was full of crabs and jazz. My mouth tasted of iodine. I picked up my coat and put my hand in the pocket for my phone. I had to text Cora. I didn't know what I was going to say, but whatever it was would be contrite. I could be good at contrite, but my phone wasn't there.

LOOKING FOR MY PHONE

I lost my hangover. One minute banging, one minute over. My head was clear and my senses did that zinging thing senses do when they need to run to survive. It was odd – I might have scoffed at the idea that people are welded to their phones, unable to live without them, but as soon as mine was gone, I felt adrift. Adrift? Maybe a better word would be "lonely", and I never feel lonely. I searched the apartment but found nothing, I searched again, still found nothing – searched a third time, still nothing. I thought about the evening. It was difficult, but I remembered some of it. I remembered the last time I'd seen it. It was in the restaurant, on the table beside my plate of pasta. I knew that. Then I'd put it in my pocket and gone to drink whisky in a bar. That had been my mistake. I'd watched television. I'd watched football. Then I'd texted Cora and she'd told me about her fuck-buddy – the bastard Sam. I found my shoes, grabbed my coat and went out.

I walked with my head down, along the pretty path towards Amalfi, as the sun climbed and the early gulls soared and the first fishing boats chugged across the bay. Some of them were red, but most of them were blue. I walked slowly, carefully, and I noticed everything. I was a detective or a priest, or a doctor looking for a cure. It's amazing what you see when you really look; I think this fact has already been noted by a philosopher.

I say I think it has, but maybe it hasn't. It feels like it should have been, but sometimes, when I think about philosophers, I have to stop myself thinking.

I found three crushed cans, one of those little butterfly clips that attach an earring to an ear, some piles of grit, a few pigeon feathers, a half-empty bottle of Peroni and a button. The button wasn't mine. A found button is a lucky button: I picked it up. It was red and had some cotton attached. I rubbed it and put it in my pocket. I passed an early walker and we greeted each other, but didn't stop to pass the time of day. I reached the place where the path flattened before the tunnels and steps to Amalfi, and stopped at the wall. I remembered this place. I remembered leaning over. I remembered spinning around and doing that pointy thing drunks do. I looked over and heard a warbling bird. I smelt bread baking and felt the top of the wall. It was rough. My hands were smooth – a writer's hands – lazy hands – lost hands – hands that need. I looked at my knuckles and then I saw my phone. It was lying on the terraced ground, twenty feet below me, beneath a lemon tree.

The wall was a sheer drop. On the other side of the terrace was a wire fence and, beyond this, a house. Smoke was coming from its chimney and clothes were hanging on a line. Some bits of a motorbike were leaning against the side of a knackered shed. Twenty yards along the path, a narrow flight of steps led down towards the house. I didn't think. I passed a sign that read "*Attenti al cane – e al padrone!*" I walked on until I reached a small yard. I didn't stop. On the far side of the yard was a small wooden gate, and a path that led past the knackered shed and up towards the terrace and the lemon tree. To my right, the back of the house was quiet and still. Then it wasn't quiet. I heard someone run a tap and clatter some cups – cups or bowls – either or both. The back door opened – an old woman appeared. I ducked back. She threw a bowl of water towards the terrace, then closed the door. I didn't wait. I crossed the yard, ducked under the windows, reached the far corner of the house and started to walk up the path towards the lemon tree.

Love or passion or gold or fear or jewels or lights or gardens or the sun or the smell of basil or old women or water or need – all these things do good things to your mind. They hold hands and stroll together, and give you power beyond aim. They give your walking an easy swing, a twist and a cup of coffee. They become a milkman in the morning, a telescope with a view of a place you think you know, and courage beyond the steps you thought you could take. They allow you to step over walls without thinking, spot obstacles from fifty feet away and make light work of rocks. They won't help you achieve nonsense or feats of magic realism – they won't allow you to fly to a lazy imagination where you can be a rock or listen to swans talking about the scriptures or walk through fire to meet Castellani the red-winged horse – but they will give you strength. I didn't try to hide as I walked up the path. I put it in my mind that I was meant to be there, and when I reached the lemon tree, I ducked beneath its branches, stepped to where the phone was lying and picked it up.

I wiped it on my trousers, flicked it on and stared at the screen. Three texts. I'd read them later. I put it in my pocket and turned around. I took a step back down the path and, as I did, the back door opened again, a man yelled something incomprehensible and a dog the size of a small horse lumbered out of the house and sniffed the air. It sniffed the air and then sniffed the path, and its ears pricked. It looked at the door and then looked towards me. I couldn't see if it narrowed its eyes, but it knew exactly what it had to do next.

I remember reading somewhere that although humans can read and dogs can't, a dog's sense of smell is 10,000 times more acute than a human's. So although this one might not have been able to kick back in the evening with Dante, it could smell the traces of everywhere I had walked. It could smell Naples, Rome, the ruins of Amalfi's paper mills and it could probably could smell further back. Maybe it could smell the carpet in Cora's flat, the inside of my wardrobe, the floor of a London bus, the concourse of Waterloo station and the pavements of Bermondsey. Maybe it was smelling so many confusing smells it would be confused for long enough to allow me to grab the ladder I saw lying on the ground by the wall. I lifted it upright, let it rest against the wall and stepped on the bottom rung. It snapped. The snap coincided with the dog's first bark, and then it started to run up the path towards me. I stepped on the next rung. It didn't snap. I tapped my pocket. I felt the phone and then, as the barking really started and the back door of the house opened again and the man came out to look at what the noise was all about and he saw the dog bounding up the path towards me and he shouted "*Ladro!*" and I took the next rung and I looked over my shoulder and my shoulder told me not to do that because the dog was running fast, I shot up the ladder like I had been stuck in the arse by a stick.

145

Another rung broke. I hit my chin, climbed three more, grabbed the top of the wall, pulled myself up, heaved myself over, fell on the path and lay on my back. I saw the sky. I watched an aeroplane. It was high. Rome to Cape Town? Paris to Mauritius? I cared, but I didn't. I lay for a couple of minutes while the dog barked and the man yelled about lemons and the police and knowing who I was and where I lived, and then I rolled over and crawled for twenty yards until I reached a bend, and then I got up and crouched until I was past the next bend and the barking and shouting was dim and I could stand and run down the path to a place where I knew I was safe and could stop to catch my breath. I stood up and looked at the lovely view, waited for a minute and then walked on like a man who was innocent of everything except laughing at God.

When I reached the apartment, my neighbour was sitting on his step, stroking his beard. I said "Good morning" and he wished me all the blessings in heaven, and I went indoors. I went to the kitchen, made coffee and sat on the terrace to drink.

LIVING ON THE TERRACE

I could have lived on that terrace with my coffee, the view of the town, the headland and its lemon groves, the sound of gulls, the chug of fishing boats, the little knots of men sitting outside the cafés by the beach, the smell of tomato sauce wafting up from the kitchen in the apartment below, the sound of someone playing a piano, the clang of the bells tolling from the church. I could have been a poet. I could have stayed there as my head cleared and the coffee did its work – and I read Cora's texts.

The first was a single "?", the second "Pissed again?" – the third "You said you'd call. If you can't be bothered, don't bother."

I scrolled for her number and, as my finger hovered over it, the evening came back. I could do nothing about it. I let it swamp me, and then I let it fall away. Then I let it swamp me again and I rang her and listened to the ringing as it echoed down the line from wherever she was sitting – her office? – her kitchen? – a street? – Sam's bed? Whatever. She picked up.

"Yes?"

"It's me."

"I know. Your name comes up when you call."

I let her think for a moment, to consider what she'd done, and then I said: "How's Sam?"

"She's fine. And how's your head?"

Cora could do this. When we were together she did it all the time. Or maybe I did it to myself.

"Look," I said, but then I couldn't think of anything else to say.

"Look what?"

"I…"

"You thought Sam was a man."

"I…"

"Didn't you?"

"And that while I was making love with her, I was making love with a him?"

"I'm…"

"You're what?"

"I'm…"

"You're a fool, Matt. It's that simple."

"Thanks."

"My pleasure."

Now there was one of those ticking silences that could be coloured. They might be scarlet or they might be purple, but they're not green. She sniffed. I said: "You know what?"

"What?"

"I'm sitting on a terrace. Well, a balcony, really."

"Are you?"

"Yes."

"And apart from demonstrating that you can pivot, this means what?"

"I'm drinking coffee and I've got a view of the town. There's a rocky headland in the distance and gulls are crying, fishing boats are heading across the bay, men are drinking in the bars by the beach and someone's cooking lunch in the apartment below me."

"And?"

"And someone's practising the piano. They're not bad. Not concert standard, but close…"

"Good for them."

"I just wanted to give you an idea, a flavour, something…"

"And why did you want to do that?"

"Why did I want to do that?"

"Yes."

"Because…" I said, but I didn't know. I say I didn't know, but I did know. I knew. It was obvious and sad and stupid, and as the bell from the church rang again, I said: "I'm sorry I didn't call."

"Of course you are."

"I fell asleep."

"What was it? Wine? Beer?"

"Whisky."

"Whisky. Matt. You know you can't drink whisky. You know what it does to you."

"It did it last night."

"You idiot," she said, but she didn't mean it like she could have. I heard a catch in her voice, as if she might care about what it did to me.

"I know," I said.

"You'll be useless all day."

"You know…" I said, but I stopped myself.

"I know what?"

I knew what I wanted to say. "Cora?"

"Matt?"

"I think…"

"You think what?"

"I think I've had enough of this place."

"And what does that mean?"

"Maybe I should come home."

"You call your flat a home?"

"Someone has to," I said, and as I waited for her to say something, I heard the sound of a door opening and then other people talking – office sounds, a police siren, a phone ringing.

"I think," she said, "that I already fired you once this week. Maybe you should think about that before you get on the next plane."

"I've been fired before."

"Are you listening to me?"

"Of course I am. But I wish…"

"You wish what, Matt?"

"I wish I could talk to you."

"You are talking to me."

"Properly, Cora. Face to face. I want to sort things out. You know. Between you and me. I feel like, you know, we're in limbo. Or something." I drank some coffee. "Did I tell you I'm writing a poem for you? I really am."

"You did."

"It's going to be a good one."

"Tell me, Matt. What do you want?"

"I don't know."

"Then what is there to talk about?"

"I don't know. Do I need to want something before I talk to you?"

She laughed. "It wouldn't be the first time."

"I think I'd like to talk about us."

"Us?" She made a sound that was almost a laugh. "Matt?"

"Yes?"

"Go and do some work. If you work out what you want to say, phone this evening. Otherwise, forget it."

NEXT

Scientists scoff at the idea of precognition, but I scoff at scientists with their microscopes and their understanding of natural laws, and their trousers that are always too short.

I've met dogs who know their owners are returning ten minutes before the car pulls into the drive. I've read stories about cows that lie down half an hour before the rain starts to fall, and watched cats that sense birds even though they're asleep – pigeons who know when a peregrine is a mile above them, and pilchards that sense the evil dolphin through their scales. I've known women who want to give birth in a tank full of dolphins, but I never met anyone who wanted to give birth in a cage of tigers. But tigers are so cuddly and stalky, and when they growl they sound like music, and dolphins are rapacious psychos who don't really smile.

When I was twenty-five, I went out with a woman called Sally who claimed to have premonitions. I say this now, but when we were going out I was the scientist. I scoffed. I ordered a pint. She shook her head. I patted her leg. She slapped my face. I knew my own mind and I thought I knew hers, but I was twenty-five and I knew everything. I knew how to magic metal from plastic, the sea from rocks and breasts from bras. I thought I was everything a twenty-five-year-old boy could be, and everything a twenty-five-year-old boy has ever been.

But I was wrong, and when Sally told me she'd met someone called Derek, I didn't argue. Derek had a VW bus and was driving overland to Australia. Derek had read Nietzsche and Derek had met Captain Beefheart, and Derek could speak Norwegian. "Off you go then," I said, and I went to the pub, drank myself stupid, went home, fell into bed, woke up in the middle of the night and remembered something Sally had said before she left. "One day, you're going to get into a lot of trouble over someone." Yes, I thought, genius. Thank you so much. But that was then, and now I was more tolerant of the unexplained. So when, as I sat on the terrace and thought about making some fresh coffee, I heard a bang from the bathroom, I already knew. I got up and went to investigate. The boiler, a rusted cylinder on the corner of the room, was making a wheezing sound, and water was dripping from a fractured pipe that led from the tank on the roof. I grabbed some towels, piled them on the floor beneath the leak and tried the shower. Nothing. I went to the kitchen and tried the taps. They gurgled a spit of water, then shook and made a deadly rattle. I stared out of the window. The view was very beautiful, and when the church bells chimed the half-hour, I was already missing them. But this was it. The decision had been made for me. I called Arabella. Her phone went to voicemail, so I took a deep breath and left a message.

"Hi Arabella. This is Matt from the apartment. I'm not sure your plumber did any good – something's happened to the boiler in the bathroom, and the tank on the roof is leaking. There's no water coming from any of the taps, so I'm going to have to move out and find somewhere else to stay. I'm up to date with the rent, but if I owe you anything, let me know. Thanks for everything…" I said, and I thought about saying something else – anything else – but I didn't. I hung up, went to the bedroom and started to pack. It took me half an hour. I put the key on the sitting-room table, took a last look around and stepped outside. I left the door on the latch, stood on the outside step for a moment, looked both ways, turned right and walked down the steps to the village.

TO MAIORI

I still had an itinerary, places to go, sights to chew and note-books to fill, and when I got to the bottom of the steps, I had choices. I could catch a bus, but I saw a taxi parked by a café, its driver chatting to a fisherman. "Can you take me to Maiori?" I said.

"Sure. *Salta dentro.*"

I jumped in.

Maiori was a few kilometres along the coast, and gave me options. Once we were moving, I called Cora. She was on her way to a meeting, so our conversation was accompanied by the sound of her heels clacking along a corridor.

"Hey..."

"Hi."

"I've had some trouble at the flat. The boiler packed up, and there's water pouring through the roof, so I've left."

"Bloody hell. Are you OK?"

"Yeah. I needed to leave anyway. I was getting stuck."

"OK. Where you going?"

"Not sure. I'm on my way to Salerno now, and then I think I'll head to Apulia."

"Let me know when you get there, will you?

"Of course."

The heels stopped, and I heard a door squeak open. Someone said her name, she said "Morning…" and then to me: "I've got to go. Laters, OK?"

"Sure," I said, and she hung up.

I settled back and was watching the sun on the sea when the driver said: "You need Salerno?"

"Yes, but I want to spend a few hours in Maiori."

"I can wait."

"No, please. It might be longer."

"You can take your time."

"No, really. Thank you anyway."

The driver shrugged. "OK," he said, and he turned the radio on and listened to someone talking about football.

He drove fast. I liked that. I rolled down the window, allowed the wind to chill my skin and tried to imagine what it would like to be a bird. Free as a bird? I wasn't sure. More like "constantly terrified as a bird", probably. Unless you're a raptor, I suppose, and then all you have to watch out for is a gun, but as your instinct isn't programmed to understand what a gun is or what the threat behind a trigger is, you fly on.

When we reached Maiori, the driver dropped me outside a restaurant. It was empty, and its striped awnings were faded. I stood on the pavement and stared at the sky. There were clouds high above me, and they moved slowly. I counted them. There were eight. They could have been cheese. I tipped the driver a ten and strolled towards the beach.

Maiori's pride is the longest beach on the Amalfi coast, a sweep of grey sand that curves from a rock promontory to a small

marina. In high season, this is a place of crowds and bustle,
ranked sunbeds and buzzing speedboats. Visit in February,
and it'll be you and a few well-wrapped locals who stroll
the promenade and press noses against the shuttered shops
and restaurants. An air of neglect and abandonment hangs
over the town, but it's a good air, something like the air that
hangs over an English seaside resort in winter. For scratch
the surface, and you'll discover a huddled happiness about
the place, a secure knowledge that the place is enjoying its
sheltered flipside, days of silence and reflection...

There are only so many things you can say about an Italian
seaside resort in winter, and I knew I was repeating myself. Or
was I? I crossed the road to the bus stop. Twenty minutes later I
was riding a bus to Salerno, sitting with my head leaning against
the window, and I thought about the poem I was writing for
Cora. It was about not being an atom. It was about deep things,
the sort of things that tip tables.

Once Cora told me what I should do – what I should really
do – what I should do if I was serious about writing something
serious. She said: "Take one of those creative-writing courses.
They're everywhere." I told her that I believed creative-writing
courses homogenize students and emasculate teachers – and
anyway, you can no more teach creativity than teach someone
how to breathe in a vacuum. "You're either born with it or
you're not."

"You believe that?"

"Of course. OK, maybe you can be taught the nuts, but you
can get those from a book. You can't be taught the bolts, the

style or the voice or the discipline, or any of the other important things."

"And that's why you're such a success?"

"Success is just a word."

"And you're good with words."

"Thanks."

I got off the bus at the stop before the station and walked the
rest of the way. I stood on the opposite side of the street and
watched for ten minutes. A smart policeman wandered around,
and the usual knots of ruffians and bewildered drunks. I crossed
the road and looked at the departure board. The next train to
Barletta was in half an hour. I bought a ticket.

As I was waiting, I bought a couple of postcards from a kiosk
and drank a coffee. I watched a man and woman argue about
his friends. Every time he tried to say something, she hit his
shoulder with the flat of her hand. At one point, he took out
his phone, but the moment he did this she slapped it out of his
hand. It spun through the air and, as it hit the ground, it shat-
tered. Pieces of plastic flaked and caught the sun. The sky was
very blue and the air was cold, and the smell of bread drifted
through the station.

THE TRAIN

My seat was in a quiet carriage, and as we travelled north I made a cushion from my jacket, rested my head and dozed. I had a half-dream. I was in Ireland. I met Muhammad Ali. He was alone, sitting in the corner of a low bar. I bought a drink and went up to him, and although he was shaking with Parkinson's, he took my hand and told me he wanted to read my palm. His own hand was huge and scored with deep scars, and warm. But before he had a chance to tell me what the future held for me, I woke up. The train was travelling through a cold, high landscape, sometimes through tunnels and sometimes through empty towns. I took out my notebook, scanned the pages and found a place where I'd started to write about Salerno.

Salerno in the morning. The city is a survivor. The place was devastated by the fighting that followed the Allied invasion of 1943, but its hidden gems are well worth seeking out. The Museo Pinacoteca Provinciale boasts some fine paintings by Sabatini, as well as a more contemporary collection of work by artists who made Salerno their home. The Norman cathedral of San Matteo contains – it is claimed – the remains of its dedicatee, and its Moorish (check) courtyard offers an oasis of ancient calm…

I couldn't think of anything else to say about the place, so I thumbed back a few pages, found the poem I was writing for Cora and wrote some more lines – hard lines, but soft – wrung with blood and iron, and meant. Then I put the notebook away and stared out of the window.

SHARING THE WORLD

I changed trains at Caserta and, an hour later, outside a place I forgot to notice and didn't bother to write down, the train stopped for no reason. It jolted, made a sound like an old man sighing in front of a television, and then went quiet.

The line ran through one of those edge places that lie between cities and the country. You can see them anywhere. Mysteries, tucked into the world like a bookmark you might find in a book you've bought in a charity shop, one with a torn edge and someone's name written across the top. Faded and smelling of dust or lavender, a signal sent from a stranger's home to another. And outside, through the streaked glass, a stretch of rusted wire, some cracked concrete, an expanse of scrub, a crooked wooden shed with numbers on the side. In the distance, some houses and, around them, small gardens – a road with no cars, a hoarding with a poster for a circus that passed through years ago. Wherever we were looked like the line from a song sung by a middle-aged man with a beard.

I took out one of the postcards and wrote some words to my mother. She used to be a primary-school teacher, and used to enjoy travelling. Now she lived in Broadstairs, in a flat with a lovely iron balcony and a view of a benched park and the sea, and although she was seventy-six, she hadn't given up. She read, she played canasta and enjoyed rearranging her ornaments.

Sometimes, when I visited, I took her for a walk along the beach, and she would look for stones with holes in them. "Lucky stones for a lucky girl," she'd say.

Dear Mum, Here's a picture of the Amalfi Coast, where I'm working for a few weeks. I expect you remember it from 1965. It's cold, but not as cold as the weather I hear you're having. I hope Mrs Babinski is still looking after you and you've got some of those M&S meals in. Take care. Much love, Matthew.

I wrote another to my sister. She lives in Devon with a husband and kids. She's a GP's receptionist, he works for the Environment Agency. She knows more about a patient's symptoms than the doctor she works for, and he thinks John Lennon was a genius. They never buy food that was produced more than fifty miles from their home, and their kids go to a Steiner school. Once, after we'd argued about Kenyan green beans and Peruvian asparagus, and the fact that eighty per cent of the parts in her 4 x 4 had been manufactured in Korea, I told her she was a self-satisfied snob and Steiner was a racist, and she countered by not talking to me for two years. But then she discovered Buddhism, offered me her forgiveness and sent me some beads that had been blessed by the Dalai Lama. OK, so they'd been put on a chair the Dalai Lama had sat on, but that's enough for Buddhists. Anything is enough for Buddhists, and so is nothing, which is why they're wired and never eat anything with a face. I told her I didn't accept her forgiveness, but maybe, one day, I would forgive her. Meanwhile, I said, I would tolerate her intolerance because she was my sister, and I felt guilty about putting flying ants in her pencil case when she was twelve. She countered by telling me that she didn't want to talk to me ever again, and if I had anything really important to say, I should communicate through our mother. I wish I could be as discontent as a Buddhist from Totnes.

Sue, Tom and kids! Amalfi, Naples, Rome, now heading east. It's COLD! Hope all's well with you. Much love, Matt.

I tucked the postcards into the back of my notebook, sat back and stared out of the window. The glass was smeared. The train made ticking sounds. A cat appeared from the wooden shed and started stalking towards the scrub. Birds flew up. A dog barked, and a goat appeared in the doorway of a barn. I had a thought. It was one of those thoughts that's banal but seems – at the time – so pure and perceptive. I thought it's a miracle we share the world with so many animals, yet none of them seem to know what we're doing to their world. Or maybe they do, and they're just waiting for Buddhists to arm themselves. I wrote this in my notebook, and then, as the cat disappeared behind a low wall, the train started to move.

BARLETTA

If you want to escape to the Italy Italians visit for their holidays, the south-east of the country is the place to see. Although some spots have been taken over by second-home buyers, and unchecked concrete sprawl disfigures the suburbs of many towns, Apulia hides some of Italy's finest undiscovered gems. And you can be sure that whatever the season and whatever the weather, you'll be able to find sunshine in the fabulous food and gorgeous wines the region produces.

I had a good run of clichés in Barletta. I felt free and wandered the streets with relief. Relief. Is it an emotion? Whatever it is, emotions come and go, and sometimes they simply lie down and snooze for a while. I like it when my emotions snooze.

I snapped a photograph of the famous bronze Colossus and took a pleasant turn around the Palazzo della Marra, a baroque mansion with galleries dedicated to works by Giuseppe De Nittis, a painter from the town who, some claim, was the only Italian impressionist. I don't know about that, but I do know he was a genius at painting temperature. If it's snowing in one of his scenes, you shiver, and if the sun is shining – as it does in *Breakfast in the Garden* – you want to take your coat off and mop your brow. I sat in front of it and was considering how the artist had managed to put himself in the picture without being in the picture, when my phone rang. I answered it, managed to say "Cora…" but didn't get any further. A huge woman with black eyes appeared from nowhere, hissed and pointed at a sign of a mobile with a red line through it.

I shrugged, whispered "Ring you back" into the phone, grabbed my bag and left De Nittis to himself. I found a bar with a view of the sea, ordered a coffee and phoned back.

"So, where's my poem?"

"It's not finished."

"Why not?"

"Poetry's hard-won, Cora. You've got to bleed for it. This isn't copy. You can't just knock it out."

She laughed. "It's good to know you can still talk crap."

"That's a tad harsh."

"Harsh but true, Matt. And probably a bit too late."

"What's that supposed to mean?"

"Weren't you meant to write me a poem when we were together?"

"Does poetry conform to what's meant?"

She laughed again. "Pretension suits you."

"Thanks."

"You'll be writing haiku next."

"I might do that."

"I look forward to it."

I heard the sound of a phone ringing, and the sound of a teaspoon rattling against the side of a mug.

"So," I said, "why did you phone?"

A moment's silence, one of those moments you think might mean more than the sum of its parts.

COUNTRIES

When I tell people what I do, they sometimes suck air, shake their heads and ask: "So where do you go on holiday?" And I say: "Suffolk." They don't believe me, but that doesn't bother me. It's difficult to convince most people that travel doesn't necessarily mean holiday, and writing a guide book is mostly about telling the unimaginative what to do and what to avoid, and a list of instructions for people who can't be bothered to work it out for themselves. And then, after they've told me that Suffolk does have some interesting sights, they sometimes ask: "Where would you like to go that you haven't been?" And I say: "Japan." Then they say: "Why Japan?" And I tell them that I want to surround myself with a language I don't understand and never will, get lost in a culture that meets all my expectations of what culture should be, and I want to apologize for stealing the haiku. I want to prostrate myself before Basho's tomb and place flowers on Ryōkan's, and throw the torn pages of *Writing Haiku for Beginners* by Patricia Holst into the waters of Lake Saiko. Thinking you can write a haiku in English is like thinking you can catch a fish using a ribbon of smoke. OK, feel free to write a three-line poem, but don't call it a haiku. Call it a fewtio, a drore or a wantoroy, but don't call it a haiku. Don't confuse an English syllable with a Japanese *on*, and don't confuse your ability to concentrate for more than twenty-five minutes with a genius for writing short verse. Or, as I wrote on a bus once:

"Cultural imperialism,
appropriating another
country's treasure."

So I went off on one there, but these things need to be said. Cora used to accuse me of going off on one for no reason, but I used to tell her that I always had a reason, and what's the point of living if you don't feel passionate about some things. "Yes," she said, "but there's being passionate and there's being an irrational arsehole."

THE GULLS OF BARLETTA

"So," I said, "why did you phone?"

A moment's silence, one of those moments you think might mean more than the sum of its parts. It hung in the air like the smell of fish, and then the gulls of Barletta cried through the sky, and one of them spotted some bread in the road. It swooped down, took its prize and flew to a steep roof to eat.

"Do I need a reason to phone one of my team?"

"I don't know. Do you?"

"No. I don't. Or someone I like to think might be a friend."

"Oh, Cora. I didn't know you cared."

"Of course I do."

"I was thinking the other day – about how you used to call me an irrational arsehole."

"And?"

"That's it."

"Proof positive," she said, and she cackled. She used to cackle a lot, especially when she knew she was right about something. "Where are you?"

"Barletta. Trani tomorrow, then Molfetta."

"Nice. You know, sometimes I miss being on the road."

"You could join me for a couple of days…"

"I don't miss it that much. And with our history, well, think about it, Matt?"

I thought about it and said: "Cora?"

"Yes?"

"Did you know?"

"Did I know what?"

"When the Japanese mend a broken vase, they aggrandize the cracks by filling them with gold."

"And why do they do that?"

"Because they think that when something's been damaged, when it has a history, it's more beautiful."

"Interesting."

"Isn't it?"

"So… Am I more beautiful because of our history? Or in spite of it?"

"Cora," I said, "you'd be beautiful with or without our history."

"And you," she said, "you're cracked."

TRANI

I slept well in Barletta. The bed was wide, the curtains were thick, the air was scented with a recent guest's perfume and I dreamt I was married to Roberta Flack. It was good being married to Roberta Flack, and we got on well, but she spent a lot of time on the telephone, organizing tours and personal appearances. She also kept asking me if anything she'd recorded since her first album had matched that work's spontaneity and genius. She didn't believe me when I told her that everything she did was touched by genius, but when I insisted it was true, she leant towards me and stroked my face and said: "You're my special man." I suggested that could be the title of a song, and she nodded, looked for a pen and paper and wrote the line down. "You're my special man..." she said, and she tapped her pen against her chin, "who knows his baby..." And she smiled.

When I woke up, I felt fresh and clean, and after breakfast I took a bus to Trani. By the time I'd found a quiet table in a clean café, I was ready to write something special. I don't know if I succeeded, but I did try.

Of all the towns along this section of the east coast, Trani is probably the finest. The medieval streets shine, the busy harbour bustles with a fleet of colourful fishing boats, and every house is a jewel in this Apulian crown. You'll be lucky to find a cathedral with a more beautiful setting, and if you find it open, it's worth taking a look at the amazing bronze doors that used to grace the entrance. But of all the treasures of the town, none is more amazing than the castle. It was built in 1233, but at first glance, it appears to have been designed by a Slovakian Cubist (check), and restoration has brought back its limestone walls to a shimmering, blinding white. During the season it serves as a celebrated and popular performance space, but in the winter months, as the wind whips the waves against its walls, the empty halls and the beautiful central courtyard can echo to no one's footsteps but yours and those of the ghosts of the Swabian soldiers who patrolled its ramparts.

I saw a pair of ghosts once. I was staying in a country hotel in Somerset. I was freelancing for a Sunday broadsheet, and had been commissioned to write a piece that was to be included in a spread headlined (not by me) "The Cosiest of the Cosy. We visit the Hidden Hotel Hotspots of the West Country".

After a pleasant meal and the opportunity to taste a selection of single malts, I retired for the night. I'd been given a room at the top of the hotel, at the end of a narrow corridor. "The old servants' quarters," said the manager. "They're very atmospheric. I think you'll like them."

The ceiling was low and the windows were small, but the bed was comfortable and the bathroom featured an excellent selection of premier toiletries and a pile of soft white towels. I suppose I should have known. Maybe I did, but I forgot to remember whatever guesses I made. I wrote some notes about the meal, read a magazine about the attractions of the area, turned out the light and settled down for the night.

The pillow was soft. I'd reached that moment when your consciousness lets go and the edge of a dream nudges in. It was going to be a light dream, probably something involving ducks and a rowing boat on a lake. I heard a faint scratching. For a moment I thought it was coming from the start of the dream, but then it was above my head. It stopped. It started again. It had moved to a place by the window. It came back towards me, stopped and didn't start again. Silence slipped down. I imagined a cloud, a mist, the dip of oars into a flat lake, the slap of water, the call of low birds. An old hotel was going to have a mouse or two, so I turned over, let the dream come and fell asleep.

Two hours later, I woke up sweating. The room was warm, and I heard a buzz in the air. I lay awake for a couple of minutes, then got up and went to the bathroom for a glass of water. I opened a window and, as I headed back to bed, a woman said "Thank you…" in my ear. She said it so close that I felt her breath on my cheek, but when I turned towards the direction of her voice there was no one there. I said "Hello?" but no one replied. I said "Hello?" again. I waited to feel scared, but I didn't. I waited for a chill, but no chill came. I got back into bed, stared at the ceiling for five minutes and turned out the light.

I tried to sleep, but opening the window hadn't made a difference. I was still too warm. The scratching started again, this time from somewhere near the wardrobe at the foot of the bed. I sat up, and for a moment thought about ringing reception with a vigorous complaint. I had my hand over the telephone when something shivered by the wardrobe. The air twitched and took on a shape. First a pillar, a column if you will, bent at the bottom and swollen at the top. It turned as a Christmas decoration turns as it's taken by a draught, and then snapped into a human shape. It radiated its own light, gave off the smell of oranges, made no sound. I wasn't scared, but I was intrigued. I'd read somewhere that ghosts are projections from your mind, thoughts given physical presence, so I suppose I wondered if this was an old friend come to visit, and when the face became more defined and I was looking at a woman, I tried to remember if I knew her from somewhere.

I'd known women. I'd known good women, bad women, mad women and women who could not let go. One of these women had lived for three months in Mexico, and some had believed in God. One used to play darts, and another used to swear in Latin. I knew a murderous Hindu and a small Canadian who only ate fish. This ghost woman had long blond hair, a thin face and stick arms, and I didn't recognize her from anywhere. She moved slowly and, as she did, I could see her knees moving beneath the material of her nightdress. She was six feet away when she stopped and turned her head. She looked towards the window. I looked towards the window. I heard clicks, like the clicks a wren makes as it hops after bugs. There were no birds there, but I flushed with the cooling you might feel in the moment before your plane goes down. I blinked and heard the sound of metal against stone. And floating outside, looking in the window, his eyes watered with bloodied tears, was the disembodied head of a moustachioed man. A scar ran down his cheek. He turned to look at me, and then he looked at the woman. She took a step back. I reached out for the light. My hand froze over the switch. A bell tinkled. The smell of oranges hung, the heat was steady, the head stayed where it was and the woman moved towards it. I opened my mouth. I wanted to say something. I tasted salt, and the bell tinkled again. I forced my hand to move to the light switch. I found the light switch. I pushed it. It made a click, and in the moment between darkness and light, the head at the window and the woman turned to look at me. Their eyes were full of longing, and their faces looked so sad that I thought, as I sat up in bed and stared around the empty room, that I had committed murder. But I was innocent and still too warm, and my teeth were singing with pain.

I wasn't afraid, but I didn't want to see the faces again, so I left the light on and slept badly. In the morning, as I sat down for my breakfast, I told the manager about my experience, and he told me the obvious banality. Two hundred years ago, a servant girl had been seduced by an army officer. He had promised to return from war, but had died in a muddy battlefield. She waited for years, and his slaughtered face was all she had to remember him by. Every now and again, a guest saw the lovers. "We don't advertise the story," he said. "We don't want to encourage weirdos."

"Quite right," I said, and I ordered scrambled eggs. Later, as I was leaving, I stole a pepper mill, but that's another story. Actually, it's not another story: it's simply a tedious anecdote.

FALLING OVER

I fell over in Trani. The streets were slick and I turned a corner too quickly. As I went down, I heard a seagull cry, and as I sat up and leant against a wall and rubbed my knee, I had the idea that the gull had caused me to fall. I looked up, but it had flown away. There was no one around, so I stayed where I was and felt sorry for myself. Then I stood up, brushed my trousers and went to look for lunch.

I found a place with a view of the harbour and the castle, ordered risotto, opened my notebook and flicked through the pages.

It was a mess, but I didn't need to be told. There was too much going on. Here were a few lines of a poem, there some paragraphs of a kids' story, here an idea for a novel, there scribbles about random Italian sights. There were even some attempted drawings of houses and streets, the sort of thing a child would do and then throw away. My notebook was a meal at a wedding that all the guests knew would end in divorce. I took out my phone and texted Cora. "I meant what I said yesterday," I wrote, and sent it. The risotto arrived. I started to eat. A text pinged back. It said: "Remind me. If you can."

I typed: "You'd be beautiful with or without our history…" and went back to my lunch.

I suppose she got busy, because she didn't reply for an hour. I was strolling around the castle when my phone buzzed. I found a place where I could sit with my back to the old stones and a view of the sea and read: "Where are you?" I texted: "Trani. Remember Essaouira? This place reminds me of there. I like it…" And while I recalled the walk we took to the Citadel where Welles filmed his *Othello*, the phone rang and she said: "Sometimes I think you do this because you want to make me angry."

"Do what?"

"You remind me of the past, and I don't like to be reminded."

"My past is everything I failed to be."

"And who said that?"

"Fernando Pessoa."

"Maybe once in your life you'll come up with something original."

"At least I admit I'm a thief."

"But only when you're caught."

"Touché."

She laughed, and I heard her take a sip of something.

I said: "I fell over this morning."

"Hurt yourself?"

"Just my pride."

"Drunk?"

"At half ten?"

"It's been known… Jesus, I'm starting to think the sooner you get back here the better."

"I can't wait."

"I could."

"Yeah. And screw you."

"Not a chance."

MOLFETTA

I took the train to Molfetta. I sat opposite an old woman. She had a mole on her cheek, was wearing a red headscarf and held a bag on her knees, her papery fingers gripping the handles so tightly I could see the blood pulsing through the veins in the back of her hands. I smiled at her and she nodded. I asked her what she'd been doing and she said, "Shopping." She reached into the bag and pulled out a bag of onions. They looked like good onions – even I could see that – and I asked her what she was going to cook, and if she'd bought any herbs and tomatoes.

"Pasta," she said, and gave me the ghost of a smile. And of course she had herbs and tomatoes. The herbs were growing on her window sill, and the tomatoes were in a bowl on the kitchen table.

I thought about my mother, sitting in her chair with her view of the sea, her playing cards spread out on a low table, her memories of teaching mathematical tables playing havoc with her mind. She used to cook pasta, but since the day she let a pan boil dry she'd left the cooking to M&S and Mrs Babinski, her Polish neighbour. And I wondered: is there something in the Italian diet that keeps old women sprightly, or is it something to do with the headscarves they wear? I didn't have time to wonder for more than a minute, because the train slowed and pulled into the station. I said goodbye to the old woman, left her staring at the floor, walked towards the sun, found a bar and a place to sit, reminded myself that the world was a blip in the cosmic rage and took out my notebook.

Like an anxious wife waiting for her husband to return from war, Molfetta looks to the sea, and her harbour bustles with a colourful fishing fleet. The old town is a maze of streets and alleys where beautifully restored houses, hidden courtyards, unexpected views of the Adriatic and dozing dogs provide the visitor with the perfect preprandial eye feast. And talking of feasts, the town's fish restaurants are justifiably famous. Sitting almost in the sea itself, L'Adriatica is among the best. Try their fabulous langoustine – so fresh they almost crawl across the plate. And with a glass (or two!) of the delicious local wine to wash them down... (try and get more clichés into this...)

I ordered a glass of wine and thought I was lost in the words, lost in my head, lost in Molfetta and lost in whatever I was thinking about Cora. And what I was thinking about Cora would not stop nagging me, so I texted: "Cora. I never meant to be a fool."

No reply.

Half an hour later I texted: "I meant what I said about not being able to wait."

I waited ten minutes. The wine tasted of apricots. No reply.

"There's ignoring and there's ignoring."

Nothing.

"Hello?"

Nothing.

"?"

Silence.

OK.

Patience. So she was probably in a meeting. I saw her sitting in a leatherette chair, twirling a pen behind a glass door, nodding at suggestions from a bearded designer, shaking her head at someone from production who was thinking about something else, ignoring her phone and the crumbs of dust on her shoes.

I put some money on the table, left the restaurant and walked towards the harbour, and as I walked, more loss crept up on me and fingered the caves of my heart. I felt it in there, wandering and creeping about. The more I walked, the deeper the loss dropped, and as it moved, it was joined by defeat. In six months' time I would be fifty years old.

My father had his first heart attack when he was fifty-six. Strolling from his work to our home in Highbury, he'd been crossing the road outside the Tube station when he'd been struck by what he described as "a bally fist in my chest". He collapsed by the toilets where Joe Orton used to cottage, and was comforted by a couple of passers-by until an ambulance arrived and he was taken to hospital. When my mother, sister and I visited him, he looked seventy and worse than defeated, and was arguing with a nurse. "I'm a cardiologist..." he kept saying. "I know the prognosis." And the nurses humoured him and asked him to be quiet while they took his pulse. He never admitted that he'd lost anything, and although he went back to work six months later, he never recovered his health. He knew and I knew. He wasn't stupid – nor was I. I saw it in his eyes. I saw what he was wishing, but he never allowed anything but duty to get in the way of living his life.

I might be a fool and looking for something in words, but at least I know how to relieve my troubles. I found a hotel overlooking the water, stepped inside and asked for a room with a view. "On the top floor, if you have it," I said, and the receptionist checked her book. She had dark eyes and very short hair. She wasn't wearing any rings on her fingers, but a silver crucifix trembled at her throat. "Seven is free. It's small."

"Seven's my lucky number," I said.

She tapped the side of her head. "You have a lucky number?"

"I used to. It used to be nineteen…"

"It used to be?" she said.

"A long time ago."

She looked at my mouth. "Of course."

"What's your name?"

"Anna."

"I'm Matt."

"Hello Matt."

"Hello."

"You want to see the room?"

"Yes please."

I followed her up a narrow flight of stairs, past paintings of buildings and photographs of plates of food. A old leather armchair sat on a landing, and a row of plants in terracotta pots. The sound of waves – the creak of wood – stones tossed down a pipe. A spider scratched her back in a hole – bells tolled – a ring of keys rattled against a thigh.

I watched Anna as she climbed the stairs and I thought of Cora. I stopped myself. When she opened the door to the room and pushed it back, light flooded in from a low window, together with the smell of roses. Light curtains fluttered. The view was of the harbour, the boats and the lighthouse. A small cupboard stood against one wall, a table was by the window and a wide bed offered the casual snoozer an opportunity to watch the chopping ocean.

"It's perfect," I said.

"You'll take it?"

"Yes please."

"One night?"

"One year."

"One year?"

"No. I was joking. One night…"

She looked at me and wagged her fingers. "You're English."

"Yes."

Ten minutes later, I was sitting at the table, thinking I could stay in this room for ever. I could lie down, pile some books on the table, close my eyes, fold my arms and watch whatever god I chose. My notebook was open in front of me, the phone next to it, my pen next to the phone. My bag was on the floor, and a spare shirt was hung over the back of a chair. There was a painting of fields by the bathroom door, and a vase of flowers on the window sill. Nothing was wrong. All my thoughts lifted, drifted and popped in the air. I picked up my phone, turned it in my hand, looked at the blank screen and laid it onto the bed. I heard a noise in another room, a cough, a sigh, the chink of a bottle against a glass, the click of a cigarette lighter, silence. I let my travels drift and, as they did, I poured my troubles into a sack and tossed them into a lake of my own creation.

EVENING

I woke to the sound of someone singing in the street.

The notes.

Listen.

It's quiet in Molfetta, and whispers are coming from your days. They're not lost or forgotten, but they might be packed in a cardboard case, floating away from a sinking ship. Children swarming around the lights, wrecked balconies topped by luggage. The screams. The sea. The waves. The sinking string quartet, the music burgled by water. Drunk corridors. Ice flipping against portholes, the wail of the swamped engines. Stop me now. I'm going past the place where the water cracks and the music dies.

I went to the bedroom window and looked down. An old man was by the hotel door, working his way through an aria from an opera I didn't recognize. I have opinions about opera, but I didn't share them. I listened for a moment and then checked my phone. Nothing. I sat at the table, opened my notebook and flicked to the lines of the poem I'd been writing. What had I said? That you've got to bleed for poetry? You have to fight across a field? Nonsense. Anyone can toss it out. I tore the page out of the book, screwed it into a ball, lobbed it across the room, grabbed my coat and went downstairs.

Anna was sitting at the reception. As I passed her, she touched her hair and dropped a pen on the floor. As she leant over to pick it up, I said: "Thank you for the room. It's lovely."

"And the bed is good?" She put the pen on her desk.

"Very," I said.

"So you're going out for the evening?"

"Yes. Is there a good restaurant?"

She gave me a small, pitying smile and said: "They're all good."

"Of course they are." I slapped my forehead.

"You take your choice," she said, "and you enjoy…"

I found a place by the harbour, ordered a glass of wine and sat at a window. There was football on the television, but I didn't watch. The other drinkers were standing at the bar, staring at the screen, their mouths open. There was a febrile atmosphere in the place, and the commentator was hysterical. I left my drink on a table and went outside for some air, and as I stood and watched a man mend his nets, I saw Anna strolling by. She was walking arm in arm with a boy, and when she saw me she smiled and said: "Goodnight."

"Enjoy your evening," I said.

"We will."

When they were out of earshot, the boy said something to her and she laughed, a tinkling laugh that rose into the air and hung over the street. I watched it hang there, waited as it faded away and went back to my drink, and as I sat down, one of the men at the bar turned and nodded at me. He had no reason to nod: we were just two humans on the harbour dock. He had two days' stubble on his face and a ragged shirt. I nodded back. He turned back to the television and, two minutes later, someone scored a goal. The bar erupted. I sipped my wine, picked up a menu and studied it for a couple of minutes. I chose *risotto alla pescatora* and, while I was waiting for my food, I opened my notebook and scribbled a few lines about the view. Then I stared at my knees.

ARABELLA

I'd been considering the miracle of my knees for a few minutes when my phone rang. I looked at the screen. I didn't recognize the number but it was Italian. I don't usually answer numbers I don't recognize, but the wine had got the better of me.

"Hello?"

"Mr Baxter?" The voice was a woman's voice. It could have been singing at me.

"Yes?"

"This is Arabella. From Atrani."

"Oh Arabella. Yes. Hello. How are you?"

"I'm fine. And you?"

"I'm OK, thanks. Have you been to the apartment?"

"Yes. I'm very sorry about the water."

"Please. Don't worry. I'm sorry I left without saying goodbye."

"You've found somewhere else?"

"Yes."

"You're welcome to come back any time, and for the inconvenience you can stay for a week, no charge…"

"That's very kind of you."

"And I promise you'll have water. Marco is mending it now."

"Thank you."

"It would be our pleasure."

The waiter came with my food and said, "*Risotto alla pescatora?*"

"Yes," I said.

"I'm sorry," Arabella said. "You're eating."

"I'm just about to start."

"Then I'll leave you to enjoy."

"Thank you."

"But call when you want to visit us again. OK?"

"I'll do that," I said, and then she said goodbye and hung up.

MAN ON WIRE

Two hours later I lay in bed, but I couldn't sleep. I turned one
way and then the other, and once I'd gone through a night-time
parade of places and feelings and thoughts I could not avoid –
Cora's face, my childhood bedroom, a marsh in Essex, a river
in Somerset, the woman I met in Rome, a hillside in Spain,
Cora's eyes, guilt, acid in my stomach, toothpaste, Venice and
drowning – I found myself staring at a terror I sometimes face
at night. So it makes no sense, and compared to the ridiculous
it's absurd, but I can't help myself. I end up facing Philippe
Petit, a man who, in August 1974, walked a wire between the
two towers of the World Trade Center.

It's an old story, but I'll write it. It's not easy and it's not
simple, but it's true. I never used to be afraid of heights, but
one day – I caught it. So people might say you can't catch a
fear, but I'd say that all you have to do is travel to Gdańsk and
climb the tower of St Mary's Church, because your editor has
put it on a list of things you have to do. The day I did it, the first
part of the climb was up a sweep of stairs – or were the stairs a
ramp? My memory is vague about details of the experience – I
think it was a ramp – but my memory becomes sharp when I
think about the feeling that swamped me halfway up. There
was no barrier between the edge and the drop, no handrail or
bannister, and although the way was wide, when I was halfway

up I stopped, looked across at the empty air, and my legs froze. My chest constricted, and when I reached out to touch the wall, my fingers searched for something to hold on to – a tiny bump in the brickwork, a ridge, anything. There was a door ahead of me – was it a door or a simple opening in the wall? I didn't care. I went down on my hands and knees, slowly, carefully, and then I began to crawl.

I was alone and cold. My breath clouded. Each step – were they steps? – was painful. I stared at the floor, the dirt and the bricks, and when I reached the opening, I reached out and grabbed its wooden frame, held on and thanked the air.

I have no idea how I got down from that tower, but I do remember that when I got back to my hotel, I decided to shelve my idea for a travel book I'd tentatively entitled *Up Tall Things in Europe*. I'd already listed the hundred tallest structures on the Continent, but now all I wanted to do was find a bar, a table by a window and a barman who didn't ask questions.

I put my fears of heights in a locked box, but they wouldn't be still. A few years later, my friend Malcolm and I went out for a random drink and ended up eating pasta in the Brunswick Centre. It was early, and we noticed that the film about Philippe Petit's madness – *Man on Wire* – was showing at the Renoir. He said: "Let's give it a go." After thinking about it for a minute and deciding it was time to kick my fear in the throat, I said, "Yes."

An hour later, we were sitting in the dark, watching as Petit's friends strung the wire and the man changed into a pair of pumps. The film cut between stills of the day and an interview with the man as he remembered the ambition, the planning and the action – and as his eyes watered and he ran his fingers through his hair, I sank lower into my seat and wished I was blind. There was no film of the walk itself, but plenty of photographs of the man standing 1,350 feet above the streets of Lower Manhattan, with nothing but string between him and death.

I've seen horror films, but nothing like the horror of *Man on Wire*, and my fears concentrated themselves and laughed at me. They ambushed me, and although I tried to think of something else – a cup of coffee, the sun glittering on a calm sea, the smell of basil growing on the window sill of Cora's kitchen – my mind doesn't do as it's told. Petit didn't fall, and I wasn't him and never could be, but I felt his blood beneath my skin. It was too hot and quick, and I thought that the more I think, the more likely it is that he will fall – or worse: I could become him and fall.

At one point during Petit's walk, gulls flew around him, curious birds with evil eyes and beaks like knives. Sometimes they were above him and sometimes below, calling and flapping and shitting. I saw the birds, heard them, and now, years later in a narrow bed in a high room in Molfetta, I turned over and tried to think of something else. I failed. Maybe, if he had fallen, the horror would never have chosen me: his tumbling body would have been a double release. But no. He stayed where he was, threatening me in his poorly chosen trousers and going on to become artist-in-residence at the Cathedral of St John the Divine, New York City. I turned over again, and this time I managed to force my mind to think about the principles of wine-making, but I didn't get past grapes growing on a sunny hillside before the man was back, leaning back with the pole resting on his chest, saying things like "When I see three oranges I juggle, when I see two towers I walk…" and defying everything I try to avoid.

MORNING

I woke early. I survived the horrors of the high wire, and was feeling as relaxed and easy as I'd felt the previous evening. The sun was shining, and when I went to the window and opened the curtains, I saw a fishing boat heading out to sea. It was blue and white, and smoke was puffing from its funnel. I imagined myself standing in the wheelhouse with the skipper, chatting about sardines and anchovies. We'd drink strong coffee and, while he plotted our course, I'd watch the waves break over the bows and read something in the way the wind made patterns on the surface of the water. Then, tossing my coffee grounds into the wake, I'd head to the stern to do something important with nets and floats. Maybe the skipper was my father, maybe my older brother, maybe a friend of the family who had eyes for my sister. I didn't know. My imagination wasn't that strong. In another life, I could have been a fisherman. So it's a romantic idea, and the reality is probably more than difficult, but there's nothing wrong with a romantic idea. The boat disappeared behind the harbour wall and a scooter raced beneath the window. I picked up my phone and checked for messages. There was nothing. At another time I would have worried, but at that time and in that place I let it slide. If I had to, I'd worry later. I padded to the bathroom, had a shower and then went to look for breakfast.

The reception was empty, but the smell of coffee was drifting from a side room. I followed my nose. I found some pastries on a small table and a bowl of fruit. There were no freshly showered women in jeans looking at cheese, so I picked up a plate and a knife, and the noise alerted someone in the kitchen. I heard the scrape of feet, and a moment later an old lady appeared and asked me if I wanted coffee. "Yes please," I said, and she went to get busy.

As I was waiting, I ate a croissant and thumbed through my notebook. When I reached the page I'd torn out, I rubbed the ghosted imprint of the words I'd thrown away. I felt a shot of something in my head and went upstairs to my room. I found the screwed-up page under the bed, picked it up and went back to my breakfast. My coffee was waiting, and the old lady was standing by the sideboard looking at the bowl of fruit. I thanked her; she said it was her pleasure, and I sat down again, flattened the page on the table and read.

I'd written the first six lines, but now I had the rest, so I poured a cup of coffee, took a sip, clicked my pen and wrote.

Maybe I'd been wrong. Maybe a poem isn't hard-won. Maybe it's best to let it spill onto the page and crust there. Whatever – I scribbled for an hour, stole a couple of lines from the original, crossed them out, replaced them with new ones and, by the time I was ready for another pot of coffee, I thought I might be finished. And as if to confirm this thought, my phone pinged. A text.

"I wasn't ignoring you," Cora wrote. "And maybe I can't wait."

I replied with: "What are you saying?"

The fresh coffee arrived, and I wrote out a neat copy of the poem. I was pleased. I took another croissant from the sideboard, ate it slowly, drank another cup of coffee, stared at my phone and went back upstairs.

DREAMING

I lay on my bed and listened to my stomach. It was busy. I let it work. My phone was quiet, and then it pinged. I read: "I'm saying that maybe I can't wait to see you again. Sometimes."

I replied with: "I finished your poem".

No reply.

"Hello?"

Nothing.

"Cora?"

Silence.

"Oh please."

Blanked.

Two hours later I said goodbye to Anna. Her voice was a flight of birds. I looked into her eyes and tried to remember what it felt like to be nineteen. It was difficult, but I did remember buying records and carrying them home with the sleeve showing, and I did remember walking five miles to visit a girl I fancied only to find out that she'd given me the wrong address and the address she'd given me was an old lady's flat. I knocked on the lady's flat, and when she came to the door she asked me if I was the gardener. When I told her I wasn't, she told me that I could have a biscuit if I wanted, but I didn't want a biscuit. I wanted a hole in the world.

I wanted to say something to Anna, something important she'd remember, but I was dumb. I could feel my tongue in my mouth. It was lying there like a leaf. She didn't see herself as anyone but the person who sold me a room, and as I walked away I knew she was only looking at her phone, reading texts from the boy she'd laughed with.

I walked to the station. I was going to travel north. I'd made a choice. I found my train, sat in a seat, made a note in my book about leaving – "*Sometimes, leaving a place where you've been happy feels better than arriving in a place where you know you'll be happy…*" – stared at a wall, rested my head, wrote something more about leaving – "*Sometimes, leaving is all a thief can do to the thing he stole…*" – and then I snoozed.

As I snoozed, I dreamt I was a contract killer, and my Hollywood quirk was the fact that I was always naked when I killed. And in my dream I was on a rooftop. I watched myself from a distance, loaded my gun, took aim at my victim and watched him for thirty seconds before pulling the trigger. And during this thirty seconds, I grew an erection, so by the time the man's head exploded, everything was pointing in the same direction as my rifle. I woke with a start and an ache in my pants. I sat up, did that thing that snoozers do when they want to pretend they haven't been snoozing and took out my notebook. I couldn't find my pen, but it didn't matter. I was awake. I opened the notebook, looked at the lines I'd written about leaving, ripped them out of the book, tore them into small pieces and dropped them into a rubbish bin.

I had to change trains at Foggia, and had an hour to kill. I wandered into the town, up a wide boulevard, found a place that sold cakes, bought a cone filled with cream and sat on a bench in a park to eat. A pigeon came and stared at me and my cone for a few minutes, then got bored and flew off to look at some gravel.

Foggia isn't an obvious destination for the discerning travel-ler, and although it has been destroyed twice – first by an earthquake in 1731, then by the allied bombing of World War II – the city has a certain charm that will repay the curious. Forget the trouble that might be brewing around the railway station, ignore the ghastly modern rebuild and lose yourself in the hidden streets and alleys that radiate from the centre. (This is nonsense – do something about it.)

I had to run for my connection and caught it with a minute to spare. Then the train refused to leave and sat in the station for half an hour, waiting as the sun turned to clouds and the clouds ripped their edges to rain. My phone pinged with a line from Cora. "Sorry. Long meeting."

"No worries."

"So where's my poem?"

"I'll email it."

"When?"

"Soon."

"You'd better. What's it called?"

"'You Are Not an Atom'."

"Good spot."

"Sarky mare…"

"That's me."

WINE

Six hours later I was sitting in a hotel room in Salerno with a glass of wine, listening to the bells of a church, rubbing my arms and watching as lightning storms blew across the sea. I was cold, but I didn't care. I'd eaten pasta and an orange. I'd had a shower. Sometimes life is better when you're clean and your head is polished, and you have the time to laugh at your talents.

The wine was local. I swirled it in the glass, held it to the light and watched the colour twist. The label said it was from Tramonti and, although I have the palate of a cetacean, I could taste herbs and spices – and lemon, I think. I suppose I should have thought about it, tried to give words to the smell, the feel in my mouth, the taste, the finish. All the stuff I could know about if I gave myself a chance.

Once the preferred quaff of the Amalfi Republic's merchants, Tramonti Rosso is a dignified wine, made from tintore *and* piedirosso *grapes, traditionally cultivated in tufo-stone soil in precipitous vineyards that flourish between 250 and 500 metres above sea level, refined on fine lees and transferred to Slavonian durmast barrels for at least twelve months. The result is a bottle that amazes, ringing with an aroma of fruit that brings to mind the smell of sea-soaked driftwood on a shingle beach. The first attack is soft and light, while the*

evolution surprises with hints of rosemary, cinnamon and –
not surprisingly, but unusually – lemon, before the luscious
finish leaves long flavours of a deeper, less sharp citrus. If
a wine could be a person, this would be one of those old,
distinguished-looking men you sometimes see taking the air
on a warm Italian night, dressed in an immaculate suit – a
Missoni scarf draped languorously around his neck, his per-
fectly groomed hair shimmering in the salty breeze.

I opened my laptop. A dozen emails dropped into my inbox, then another dozen. Most of them were about insurance, cheap flights, magazine subscriptions and dental care. A few were from work, and one was from my agent. He wrote that he'd sent my book about the Caledonian Road to a publisher. "They're looking for something set in North London. Fingers crossed, eh?"

I emailed him a single line – "Fingers and toes, Bob…" – then took out my notebook, read the poem I'd written for Cora, thought about it, thought what the hell, thought about it again, stared at the floor, stared at the ceiling, stared at my fingers and started typing.

An hour later it was finished and ready to send. I say "finished" – but is such a thing ever finished? Who was it who said something about never finishing a work of art, simply abandoning it? I couldn't remember. And I wasn't pleased. I wasn't a poet, but can a poet say that she or he is a poet? I think not. It's for other people to call the poet a poet. I poured a glass of wine, sipped, let it fill my mouth, swallowed. I got a lot of grape. I stared at the song of my hands and hit the key. I waited five seconds, watched as the screen did what it had to do, closed the laptop and turned my face to the lilies of my life.

NIGHTWALKING

Once the poem had gone, I grabbed my coat, slapped a hat on my head and went for a walk. I left the hotel, turned right, took a flight of steps and followed the pavement as it wound its way past houses and balconies and washing, under arches, around corners, up and then down again. I was lit all the way by the glow of orange lamps and lights from warm rooms. The air was filled with the smell of garlic and herbs, the blare of televisions and arguments and laughter – a closed café, stacked plastic chairs, crates of empty bottles – a shadowed cat, dustbins, lovers who faded into a doorway. Beyond them, a busy road, the promenade and the sea. I walked on and strolled around a low quay to a place where I could stand and watch waves crash onto the rocks below.

It was still raining, and the lightning had moved south, sometimes illuminating the coast and the distant mountains, sometimes not.

Two hundred yards away, a pair of lights were bobbing. Someone had fished through the storm. They'd filled their nets, and their lights had burnt without oil.

One of my favourite poets is W.S. Graham. The man was born in Scotland, travelled south and west until he couldn't travel further, found a place to live, sat down, pulled a chair to a table, called for a beer and took out his pen. He believed he should live for poetry to the exclusion of everything else. Money, fame, acclaim – none of these things meant anything to him, and lesser writers lived their deluded lives behind his eyes. Someone took a photograph of him as he carried a can of paraffin along a Cornish cliff path. Look at it and tell me he's not caught between possession and theft: the fox with the hen. He had mad hair and bad teeth, and wrote a poem called 'The Nightfishing'. As I stood on the promenade and the church bell tolled, I was overcome by the coincidence of the moment, for the poem starts with a line that describes the striking of a bell on a night-time quay.

What sort of madness does coincidence come from? Where does it hide, and what angels fly to hold promise over its desperate house? And what madness draws someone towards the edge of a town, then to look into dark water and wonder about jumping? What is beyond the thought of suicide, beyond the toll of the quay night bell, its echo over the water and the lights that follow it to the edge?

I had the urge to jump once. I was on a ferry as it sailed through a November swell from Fishguard to Rosslare. I was travelling for work. I was going to write a piece about West Cork, and I was wondering why. Why was I there? Why was I so cold and the sailors so warm? Where was I going to be next year? How was I going to be paid? What was the point of the why? I was holding a glass of whisky, standing alone, gripping the rail, looking down at the cliff of the ship, watching the waves and watching the gulls fluoresce, and suddenly I knew no one would hear or know or care. I had no idea why the thought came, but it was seductive, and I did think it would be the way to go, dropping into the dark, lost without a trace, food for the fish, a good end. Slipped and final. Diesel, steel and salt. But I stepped away and closed my eyes. Like I always did. Like I stepped away in Salerno, remembering the taste of whisky, opening my eyes, turning around and walking back along the quay as the lights disappeared. They blinked and blinked again, and then they were gone.

I walked back the way I'd come, past the arguments and cooking and televisions, and stopped halfway up a flight of steps to catch my breath. I was leaning against a wall when a man opened his front door and a cat jumped out. He said "Go and catch that mouse", saw me and wished me a good evening. I said it was a perfect evening for a stroll through the town, and he agreed. Then he closed the door and left me to climb the rest of the way back to my hotel with his cat.

TEXTS

"Was that for me?"

   "It wasn't for anyone else."

   "Who did you steal it from?"

   "Why did you think I stole it?"

   "Aren't you a thief?"

   "What makes you say that?"

   "It was just a thought that came to me, Matt…"

   "I wrote it, Cora."

   "No you didn't."

   "I did."

   "Liar."

   "True."

   "So who wrote it?"

   "I did."

After a while.

   "Hello?"

   "What?"

   "You there?"

   "I might be."

   "Cora?"

   "Yes?"

   "I'm listening to the sea."

   "But you're a hack. You're not a poet."

"I know."
Five minutes.
"You there?"
Ten minutes.
Nothing.

NIGHT

I went to bed, but I had a bad night. The air was cold and the sheets were chilled. A crack in the curtains let a cut of moonlight into the room. I could see my breath. It left a marble of cloud in the air. My nose was frozen, and I couldn't feel my toes. Far below the window, cars rolled by, sirens wailed and late drinkers sang their way home. I heard my phone ping and picked it up. I stared at one word from Cora. "OK," it said. I typed "OK?" Two minutes later she replied with "So you wrote it". I replied with "Of course I did". I waited for a few minutes, put my phone next to a glass of water, said "Enough..." to the ceiling and sat up for half an hour to read about the ruins of the ancient city of Paestum. It was on my itinerary. I had to visit the place. More than that: I wanted to visit the place. The pictures showed Doric temples that were everything Doric temples should be. Stone cages, open to blue skies, frozen and gold. But – I thought – did I still have an itinerary? I had no idea. Maybe I did, maybe I didn't. I put my book on the floor, stared at the ceiling for a moment, turned the light off, pulled the blankets to my chin and lay on my side. I watched the failing night and then I closed my eyes.

I like lying on my side with a hand under my pillow and a leg tucked into my waist. I suppose it could be described as a half-fetal position or a pre-birth position; whatever it is, it gives me more pleasure than almost anything. More than the feel of a slow breeze through a grove of olive trees, or the sight of a bridge rising through an early-morning mist – or the taste of pomegranates or the feel of gold. And as I tried to find the place between awake and gone, I drifted to thoughts of a place Cora and I had visited where olive trees grew and an old man had offered us a glass of water from a spring.

It was our first holiday together, and we'd decided to fly to Barcelona, rent a car and drive without a plan. We found a village outside Girona and a room above a bar with a balcony and a view of the hills. On the second day, we headed into these hills, walked a path that led towards a bare summit and followed it until we reached a small farmhouse. It was the sort of house a child might draw, with a door in the middle and two windows – a low roof, a bench by the door, chickens dust-bathing in a dry garden. We stopped for a while and sat on a rock and looked back down the path. We could see the village in the valley below and, in the distance, a shredded haze hanging over Girona. I felt happy, and I think Cora was happy too, and as we listened to the breeze and took deep breaths of the spicy air, an old man appeared from the house, eyed us for a moment, said "Good morning" and threw some corn at his chickens. Then he shuffled over and asked us if we were going to visit the ruins. We didn't know about any ruins and told him we were heading for the summit. He said that we had to visit the ruins. They had been built by monks, and if we didn't visit them today, we might not have another chance. "They're falling down every day," he said.

"OK," Cora said. "Maybe we will."

"They're on your way," said the old man, and he disappeared into his house.

We sat for five more minutes, and were about to leave when the old man reappeared with a bottle. "Come with me," he said, and we followed him around the back of the house, down a gully and into a grove of olive trees. In the far corner of the grove was a rock terrace and, in the middle of this, a small cave. A stream of water ran from the mouth of the cave and trickled into a culvert. The old man ducked into the cave and came out with the bottle full of water. "For your walk," he said, and he gave it to Cora. She thanked him and put it in her pack, and half an hour later we were walking around the ruins the old man had told us to visit. We found the roofless outlines of cells and what might have been a dining room, and the tumbled remains of a chapel. We sat on a wall, took out the bottle of water and drank.

I'll never forget that water. It was scented of something – rosemary, I thought. It had a light fizz to it, and as I swallowed I felt a buzz, like I'd touched my tongue on one of those batteries you put in a smoke detector. I took another swig, and Cora scolded me. "Don't drink it all," she said, and grabbed the bottle, and took a longer swig than I'd had. I laughed and pinched her waist. It was that sort of holiday, the sort that sticks in your head like a spell and casts itself over the rest of your life.

I turned over in my bed, put my other hand under the other side of the pillow, pulled my other leg to my waist and thought about Cora's waist. It's small. There's not a lot of flesh to pinch. I thought about her waist and I thought about her legs, and I thought about the top of her head. The top of her head smells of almonds. I turned my head and pushed my nose into my pillow. I think I went to sleep like that.

I woke up at around half-past three. I'd been dreaming a confusing dream about a horse. I was in a town I didn't recognize, and everywhere I went I saw the horse. It was in a shop, in a park and at the top of an escalator in a department store. I reached out and drank some water, and checked the phone. No messages. I turned over and closed my eyes again. I had another confusing dream. I'd had an accident and my arm was damaged. It hurt so much I begged the doctors to cut it off. When they refused, I said I'd do it myself, and someone said: "It's your arm. You can take it to dinner if you want." Then I started crying, and in my dream I could feel the warmth of tears on my cheeks and taste them at the corners of my mouth.

I woke as dawn leaked through the curtains. I reached out for a glass of water, drank a mouthful, lay back and watched as the ceiling swam. I fell asleep again, and woke with a sword of sunlight across my face. My head hurt, and all I wanted to do was eat eggs. English eggs and English bacon. Toast and butter. Mushrooms. Maybe a sausage. No. Forget the sausage, but leave the bacon. Streaky bacon, cooked to a crisp. I rolled out of bed, used the bathroom, found a shirt, picked up my phone, opened the curtains, blinked at the day, opened my phone and read a text. It said: "OK. You're not a thief."

BREAKFAST IN SALERNO

I had a shower, got dressed and went down for breakfast. A few people were drinking coffee, but none of them were damp women. There were a pair of business people in a corner, and a man who looked like a retired bullfighter. I say this because he had a livid scar that ran from the crown of his head down his cheek to his chin. It looked like an old scar, but it still looked fresh. He walked with a limp, and when I went over to stare at the plates of cheese and ham, he joined me and said: "*Hola.*" I think his accent was Andalusian, and I know a lot of bullfighters come from Andalucía, but it would be stupid to assume every man who comes from Andalucía is a bullfighter. I'd read *Death in the Afternoon* and knew that bullfight is rooted in emotion. The emotion the crowd feel as the band play their first notes, the emotion as the cuadrilla appear, the emotion as the torero makes his first pass – the emotion of the close, the skin against the thigh, and the heat.

"Maybe I was losing it. Maybe I'd already lost it. I poured a cup of coffee, plated a couple of pastries and a banana, and went to sit by the window. I ate and drank and thumbed Cora a text – "In Salerno. Had a dream about you…" – finished the coffee, fetched another cup and stared at the rush-hour traffic as it poured into the city, and I watched an old man push a pram down the road. There was a scruffy dog in the pram, and every now and again the man stopped and picked something up from the pavement. When I was a kid, I developed a fear that one day I would become homeless and ragged, but now, older, I wonder if it was a fear or a longing. For the man with the pram looked happy, and his dog looked loved and well fed. Were the Buddhists of Totnes right? Could it be true that the sloughing-off of possessions and want is a key to contentment, and the lack of adornment is at the heart of happiness? I have no idea. I can't answer my own questions, but I can tell you that, as I was finishing my tea, the man stopped, tipped his head back and opened his arms to the sky. I don't know if he had seen a Christ in the clouds, or flights of angels ascending, or birds. But then he turned and looked towards me, and although I don't know if he could see me, for a moment I thought he was trying to say something to me.

PAESTUM

I checked out of the hotel and, as I stepped into the street, I was relaxed. This was not necessarily a good state to be in, but I didn't think I was making a mistake. I'd decided to take each day as it came, get on with the rest of the job, complete the itinerary and only make important decisions when important decisions had to be made. I'd stay in a different hotel each night – I wouldn't call ahead – I wouldn't eat in the same place twice – I'd talk to random strangers for a particular reason, or maybe for no reason at all. What I did would depend on my mood. I'd be the traveller I was meant to be, and the writer I could be. I'd take my experiences and use the alchemy of Robert Frost's idea to turn them into gold. Then I'd take the gold and feed it to the birds that old men fed in Parisian parks. It would be easier than winning a race, but longer. I stopped at a kiosk and bought a newspaper, crossed the road and found a bus stop. I was going to Paestum.

If the crowds of Pompeii and Herculaneum are too much for you but you still need a fix of the ancient, look no further than Paestum. Thirty miles south of Salerno, the ruins of this amazing city rarely attract more than a handful of visitors, and as you wander the deserted site, it's easy to imagine that you've stumbled across the place in some sort of feverish dream...

Built by the Greeks in the sixth century BC, taken by the Romans in 273 BC and abandoned in the middle ages, the place disappeared into a swamp of snakes, scorpions and malarial mosquitoes. Hundreds of years later (how many, exactly? check), the forgotten temples were rediscovered, and subsequent excavations have revealed defensive walls, an amphitheatre, wide streets, narrow alleys and the outlines of spacious homes and luxurious bath houses...

As I rode the bus, I read more about the place, and the driver dropped me at a crossroads on the edge of the modern town. I say it was a town, but it could have been a village. Maybe it was a hamlet – I don't know. I used to know the difference. It had something to do with the place having a church. There were houses and a bar, and some shops selling trinkets. I saw a church. A village? Let us call it a village.

When I asked the driver where the ruins were, he laughed and said: "You don't need me to tell you. All you have to do is look." He was fat – his eyes were like olives in bread, and his breath smelt of cheese. The bus's steering wheel pressed into his stomach, and as he watched me step onto the pavement, he shook his head and made a clicking sound through his teeth. His teeth were yellow, but I don't think he cared. A woman who'd been sitting behind him said something about Germans, but he shook his head again and said "English". "Same fools," said the woman, and then the driver pressed the button that closed the door and I was left by the side of the road with the wind and the blue sky, and the call of birds from a stand of pine trees.

I like pine trees. I like their smell and needles, and the way they whisper in their sleep. I stared at them for a minute, watched the birds rip through their branches, and then I saw a sign. I followed it, found a café and a table with a view of the ruins and ordered a coffee. When the waiter asked me where I was from, I told him I lived in Oslo, and laughed when he said I probably found the weather quite warm. I suppose it was quite warm, though a little breeze rippled the edge of the closed canvas canopy that hung over my head. The waiter went back to do something in the kitchen and, as I heard him drop a metal tray, my phone pinged. Cora. "Sorry. In another bloody meeting. Glad to hear it. About time you behaved like a proper writer."

I didn't reply. I drank the coffee and went to explore.

I crossed the road, bought a ticket from a woman at the main gate and took a path that led towards the amphitheatre. In the 1930s, engineers built a road through the site, routing directly through its centre and cutting the amphitheatre in two, but even with the destruction I felt a chill. I walked through the gate the gladiators used and stood beneath the terraces where the audience sat. The killing animals would have come from a low hole in the first tier of the wall – the crowd yelling, the sand offering no grip at all, the sun high and hot – the stench of shit and piss and vomit, the missiles from the crowd, the hopelessness of the spear, the teeth and blood. My imagination is pale and easily led, but it didn't need anything but a narrowing of my eyes in that place. Although Rome's Coliseum is one hundred times the size of Paestum's, my chill came from the intimacy of the smaller place. I don't know, but I think the best animals and the best fighters were sent to fight in the capital – this was the Roman equivalent of a second-division football ground. Half-filled, adverts for a pottery and a builder, a stall selling bad pies. I ran my fingers over the dead stones, left the way I'd come and headed towards the temples of Hera and Neptune.

These were the glories of Paestum, and although their roofs and interior walls were missing, the massive columns still stood. I wandered around them a couple of times, each time wondering if I should hop over the wooden fences that surrounded them and climb the steps to explore the places where the statues and offerings were once kept. But men in smart uniforms were lurking, men with bored expressions and walkie-talkies, and they wanted something to do. So I kept to the paths, took a few photographs and exchanged words with a German gentleman. He was sitting on a truncated column by the remains of a bath house, a feathered hat on his head, a sketchbook on his knees and a pencil in his hand.

"Hello," I said.

"*Nein!*" he said, without looking up.

I moved on and followed the ancient cobbled road to the ruins of the houses that clustered around the temples. Some had the remains of mosaic floors and marble basins where rainwater collected. The largest had small rooms where a slave could stand and greet visitors and lead them into a pretty courtyard where flowers grew, a fountain tinkled and the mistress of the house waited with a bowl of fruit. Here was a kitchen and here were the bedrooms, and a private study with a view of the back of the house next door. And here was a narrow alley that led to a row of shops, and the remains of a shrine to a forgotten god. This was a little ruined shelf in a ruined wall. I looked around. I was alone. Suddenly something was obvious, clear and bright. I stepped back, sat on the ground and closed my eyes.

EPIPHANY

I kept my eyes closed for five minutes, and let the sounds of Paestum fold around me. I let the sounds do this as if they were dresses, and as I breathed the air of the place and listened to the shifting of the ghosts that drifted in its streets, I looked into my heart. I suppose I could write that I saw nothing there, that its empty chambers echoed to the tolling of distant buoy bells and the clank of anchor chains – but I did see something. If you can call an amorphous shape something, I suppose I saw hope, maybe even the edge of a cut of redemption. Maybe I was faithless and maybe I was a lost man sailing a leaking boat into a storm, oblivious to the clouds and the danger, and the first spots of rain. So when I opened my eyes and saw nothing but the blue sky and high white clouds, I said, to nothing or no one in particular: "Tell me. What do I do?" But no reply came. The air was still, and the only sound was the high mewing of a single buzzard. Suddenly everything wasn't obvious. I had to make my own decision. It wasn't difficult. I stood up – and then, because my itinerary demanded it, I took a swift turn around the Temple of Athena, said goodbye to the woman in the ticket office and went to take a stroll around the museum.

I stood behind an American woman who pointed to a 2,000-year-old vase and said to her friend: "It's cracked." I saw some glass cabinets containing little figures, and the figure of a diving man from a Greek tomb, his feet at the wrong angle for a diver but the right angle for a painter, falling between this life and next. Either that or he was redeeming himself by casting off all the possessions he'd ever owned. The leafless trees on either side of the diver, the light curve of blue water, the high wall, the creamy ground. I moved on and looked at another picture, and another, and another – but my heart wasn't in it. I wanted to leave, stroll to the bus stop, wait for half an hour and feel the breeze on my face – and watch the high planes cut the sky.

BUS

As I was riding the bus back to Salerno, I opened the window next to my seat and held my phone in the rushing wind. I held it between my thumb and my finger. I did that up-and-down-motion thing that kids do when they've got a toy car and imagine it flying. I turned it towards me and turned it away, and watched it dip towards me. I wondered how long it would take someone to find it if I dropped it. I say I wondered, but I didn't wonder at all: all I did was think. Would it be run over by a car and flattened, and would the saved messages leak like water and drain into the ground and be found by ants and carried away to dark holes? No, they would not. I pulled it out of the wind, flicked it on and read three texts from Cora.

"Have I upset you?"

"Hello?"

"Oh all right then. I'm sorry."

I texted: "Sorry for what? Did you upset me?"

A minute later she replied with: "You were quiet."

"I was doing what I'm paid to do. I've been exploring Paestum."

"Talk later? I think we should."

"OK. Travelling north this evening."

"Nineish?"

"OK."

NORTH

Two hours later I was back in Naples. I'd thought about taking a bus to the mountains and finding a small town with a restaurant and a comfortable room over a bar, but I wanted another fix of the old city, and I wanted to get lost in the Spanish Quarter. So the guide books tell the visitor to avoid getting lost in the Spanish Quarter, but my least favourite word in the English language is "safe". I like a risk, and I like small rooms.

I found a small room in scruffy hotel. It had a balcony, and I could lean on the railing and almost touch the window of the house on the other side of the street. There was a shared bathroom on the landing, and someone had left a Bible on the bedside table. My father once told me that you should never put anything on top of a Bible. "Do that and you'll bring Satan down on your head." There was a picture of a generic Neapolitan street over a pine table, and a chair that creaked when you sat on it. Everything suited me. I poured myself a glass of water and phoned Cora.

"OK," I said. "From the top."

"What?"

"From the top. You liked the poem?"

"If I told you I loved it, you wouldn't believe me, so I'll just say it was OK."

"You loved it?"

"No. It was OK. So, where are you?"

"Naples?"

"Again?"

"I'm following my instincts, Cora."

"Is that wise?"

"Wisdom is overrated."

"No it's not."

"Sense. Now, that's what makes sense."

"Oh God, Matt. How much have you drunk today?"

"I'm sober."

"Yeah. And I'm a philosopher."

"Are you?"

"No, Matt. I'm not."

"So what are you?"

"A woman who's owed a few days' leave."

"Got any plans?"

"I'm going to take off, visit somewhere I haven't been before."

I said nothing. I let her words hang, and that's exactly what they did, revealing themselves and then disappearing behind their own shadows.

"And you?" she said. "What are your plans?"

"Palermo. I have to visit Palermo. Lots to do down there."

"You been there before?"

"Yeah. For the first edition. You?"

"No."

"So that's the somewhere you haven't been before."

"What are you saying?"

"Oh come on, Cora."

A long pause.

"Not a chance…" she said.

THE SPANISH QUARTER

I left the hotel, turned right and walked. I was feeling rough and poor, and my hands prickled. The little streets were slick and sinister, and where light came from windows and open doors, it smeared across the cobbles in dirty pools. The sky was patched with orange clouds, and no birds sang. Sometimes I could smell wood smoke, then petrol, then lemons, then something acrid I couldn't identify. I walked with my hands in my pockets. I felt clear and bright, but I had no idea where this clarity had come from. The feeling of menace that surrounded me? The idea that it's not just artists who can hold two opposing views and still function? The troubles that give life meaning?

The secret of keeping safe in a place you don't know is, as everyone knows, to look as though you know where you're going. Be the place. Don't wear an anorak. Pretend you know that door, those dogs, that window and the taste of that dish. Listen to your footsteps echoing, beware of quick movements at your side. Imagine you have a friend who lives in one of these streets and he's waiting for you to call with news about a job. Have a back story, some sort of narrative. Know yourself and your imaginary friend. I walked straight and didn't stop until I found a bar. It was a small place with faded posters on the glass door, and when I pushed my way inside, the half-dozen men who were drinking at the zinc top turned to look at me.

I nodded a polite good evening, asked for a glass of wine, carried it to a table in the corner and sat down.

A radio was playing mournful songs, and the men talked in low whispers. I caught a few words – "I told them they needed to leave the truck outside...", "All the fruit was rotten by the time we got it up there..." and "We need to speak to Mario about the holes..." – but couldn't work out what they were referring to. The barman came over with a small plate piled with triangles of pizza, and I asked for another glass of wine.

I once had an idea to write a book about peasant food. It might have been a recipe book, it might have been a history, it might have been a series of short stories with little watercolours illustrating the food – but whatever it might have been, it would have featured stuff like pasties, tortilla, pot-au-feu, clapshot, minestrone and succotash. I'd travel around the world and meet the people who cooked the food and ate it, and listen to their stories and their music. When I ate the little pieces of pizza in that warm place in Naples, the idea returned and knocked on my door. Tomato and mozzarella on the palest, thinnest skin of pastry. I took out my notebook and wrote:

Comfort could be an illusion, it could be a promise, it could be a memory or a dream. Or it could be something more tangible – a drink, a friend or a lover. But when it's a glass of Fiano and a plate of pizza margherita served in a warm Neapolitan bar on a cold night, comfort goes beyond the tangible and (what is beyond the tangible?)... The books say you shouldn't venture into the Spanish Quarter after dark, but I suggest that the only time to venture into the Spanish Quarter is after dark,

*when the streets are empty of nervous tourists and the area
surrenders to its true nature. Edgy, friendly, shadowed and
twitchy: Caravaggio would have felt at home here. Indeed, he
was at home here, protected for a few months from the fury
of the Roman authorities, who had determined to bring him
to justice for the murder of a rent boy (was he a rent boy, and
is this a history lesson or a guide book?)*

The words swirled. I looked up from my notebook and tapped
the page with my pen. Two of the men at the bar were looking
at me. When I caught their eyes, they held mine for a second,
looked at each other and turned back to stare at their drinks.
One of them was bald, and the other wore a hat. They were
drinking beer.

I looked back at my notebook, read what I'd written, didn't
care, shut the book, slipped it into my pocket and ate another
slice of pizza. Maybe I would write that book. The one about
peasant food – not the novel – or the children's book – or the
other one I had planned but couldn't remember anything about.

I stayed in that bar for one more glass and another slice of
pizza, then pulled on my coat, turned up the collar, paid the
bill, nodded goodnight to the other customers and stepped
outside. I let the door slam shut and watched as drizzle came
slow and fine, drifting between the houses and swirling around
the lights. I was sheltered by a porch, but I stepped into the
middle of the street and let it wet my head. It was cold, but not
too cold, and as it trickled over my face I heard the sound of
someone playing a piano. It came from a window to my right,
an unpractised hand, but one that loved a fugue. I know people

who love a fugue. I love a fugue, you love a fugue, she loves a fugue. I waited until the last note faded, turned right, took a slow breath and headed deeper into the quarter. I'd been walking for half a minute when I heard the bar door squeak open and slam shut, and muffled voices bounced off the walls behind me. I put my head down, and when I reached a place where four alleys intersected and a wrought-iron arch displayed a curve of black stars, I turned left and looked over my shoulder. The bald man and the man with the hat were following me, except now the bald man was also wearing a hat. When they saw me, they stopped walking, turned to each other and said something.

I'd turned into a narrow alley, so narrow that the drizzle funnelled in a concentrated, stinging torrent. My footsteps echoed, and somewhere high above me I heard a child crying. I turned right at the next split and walked up a flight of three steps that led to a small square. There was a shuttered café in one corner of the square, and a barrow with a red-and-white striped awning. I had a choice. I could turn back, go straight on or climb another flight of steps towards the sound of music and laughter. I chose the music and laughter. I found the music and laughter. It was coming from a small house with narrow windows. I stopped for a moment, slipped into a shadow, leant against a railing and watched as a family ate their dinner – a warm, happy family with plates of food, bottles of drink and things to say to each other. A young man stood up and poured some wine for the woman next to him, and then some for himself, and shook his head at the three children who sat opposite. An older man laughed and said something to the youngest child, who reached out and pulled at his moustache. The woman smiled at the child, who pulled a face and tried to look upset. A door opened, and a second woman appeared, her grey hair tied in a bun. She was carrying a bowl of food and left the door open. She'd come from a kitchen. She put the bowl on the table, patted a child's head and sat down. The child smiled, and someone I couldn't see laughed. The young man stood up and walked to the window, cupped his hands around his eyes and looked out. He was a handsome man and wore an open-necked shirt. He turned back to the room, lifted a glass and drank.

It was a cold night, but I felt warmed by this little scene, the laughter and ease, and the love. I looked over my shoulder. I didn't see anyone. A gap in a wall led deeper into the quarter. I stepped out of the shadow and walked on, and the alley was darker and narrower, and the cobbles shone like glass.

Maybe recklessness breeds recklessness – maybe risk loves me – maybe I didn't know how to gamble, or maybe I didn't care. I caught the smell of the drains: the taste stuck in the back of my throat, and a cat darted from a hole in a wall, stopped, arched its back, hissed, turned and ran ahead of me. I followed until it darted through a half-open door, and then I was in a wider alley. A scooter swerved around me, another scooter came from the other direction, beeped and disappeared. I stood against a wall and tried to work out which way I needed to go. I turned left and walked on.

I walked for five minutes and reached a corner I recognized. There was a faded Cinzano advert on a wall, a
lamp-post with posters for rock concerts, and some stacks
of empty vegetable boxes. I turned around. The two men
from the bar were standing on the opposite side of the
alley. I stared at them and they stared back, and when I
took a step, they moved towards me. As they got closer,
I felt a breeze in my legs, cold and creeping, and as it
moved towards my waist my stomach tightened. I thought
about turning and running, but they looked fit and fast.
One of them smiled at me – I didn't smile back. It was
too dark to smile.

I'd read somewhere that in the moment before death you're
less likely to see your life pass in front of you – more likely
to fixate on something random, something like a bridge, a
bed or a bucket, a garden, someone you dislike or someone you drank tea with under an apple tree – your first
pet, your last meal, a dream in which you were wandering through a forest with a woman who looked like your
second cousin. I chose to fixate on the smell of an old tent
I used to sleep in on the camping holidays I used to enjoy
when I was a kid. I have no idea why – the comfort of the
womb, the comfort of the exciting, the reassurance of an
unknown night, the pale dawn flaking through a tear in
the yellow canvas – whatever it was, I closed my eyes and
took a deep breath and smelt that mixture of damp, grass,
rubber and cotton. The routine was always the same – we'd
pile in the car and drive to the coast, where my mother and

sister would stay in a B&B while my father and I pitched two tents in a farmer's field. They'd wake to the smell of clean sheets, bacon and eggs, we'd wake to the sound of pattering rain and sheep rustling through the grass; they'd spend the day dozing or wandering around shops, we'd spend the day pretending to be Uncle Quentin and Dick. An adventure would usually start by father identifying the farmer as an escaped prisoner, or the woman in the local post office as a spy, and before we knew it, I was lost in a world where everything ended in imagined mystery and sand dunes or a tea shop.

I opened my eyes and, as the two men stood in front of me, I wondered if I could diffuse the situation by asking if they'd ever been on a camping holiday or whether there were any tea shops in Naples. I opened my mouth, but before I could say anything, the smaller man said: "Good evening."

"Hello," I said.

"You're lost?"

"I think I might be…"

"I'm not surprised. This is no place for tourists."

"I'm not a tourist."

"Of course you're not. You live up there." He pointed to a window. It was open. He looked at his friend and smiled, and his friend smiled back.

I shook my head. "No. I live in London."

"So you're lost?"

I nodded.

"Then you're a tourist."

I didn't argue.

"Where are you staying?"

I told him the name of the hotel.

"Nice. Not expensive, but clean."

"I like it."

"Who wouldn't?"

"Maybe we should come back with you and you'll buy us a drink."

The other man laughed and said: "Ignore my friend. He has no manners. He never says please."

"I always say please."

"Do you?"

"Always."

"Tell me. Tell me when you last said please."

"I can't remember."

"You said it just then," I said.

"He's right. I did."

"OK. So you did…"

"I'm sorry," I said, "but I'm tired."

"You're tired?"

"Yes."

"And you want to find your hotel?"

"Yes. Please."

The two men looked at me and then they looked at each other. I think they were tired too. The probably had to get up in the morning and drive a truck. "OK," said the one who never said please, and he pointed. "You go to the end of the street, turn left, take the next right and you'll see Via Toledo straight ahead. You know Via Toledo?"

I nodded.

"When you see it you'll know where you are."

"Thank you."

I turned and started to walk away and, as I walked, the one who always said please called after me. "Keep to the middle of the street, Mr Tourist."

I held my hand up and waved, but didn't look back.

A MORNING IN NAPLES

I slept badly. I drifted in and out of wakefulness and dreams, so the two states melded and I was in a high place where crossroads met crossroads, thieves came and soothed my brow and lovers from my distant past came and accused me of their own crimes. Half an hour after getting up and showering I was tired, but I went out and found breakfast, booked a flight to Palermo and took a bus to the docks. I had a few hours, so I wandered the streets and found a place where I could drink coffee and watch the cruise ships. They were huge, and if I closed my eyes and squinted, they looked like radiators. They were radiators – their passengers were heat – the coaches that collected them from the gangplanks were coaches. Some kids were roller-skating around a car park and, on the other side of the road, a woman was playing her guitar and singing a song. It was a sad song about a girl who waits for a sailor to return. As I listened, I thought that there must be thousands of sad songs about people who wait for someone who's not coming home. Sometimes I like to think banal thoughts. They help me keep any idea that I should live a usual life bolted and locked in a cellar.

The woman finished the song, rested the guitar on her knee, closed her eyes and tipped her head back to catch the sun. Birds flew, a dog barked. Coaches arrived to collect people from the ships. A moment later, a man pulled up in a car, wound down the window and shouted: "Maria!" The woman opened her eyes, waved to the man, picked up her guitar and ran to meet him. They kissed through the open window; she went to the passenger door, opened it, climbed in, and they kissed again. Then he wound up the window and drove away.

Sometimes I like to watch everyday things and wonder what's going to happen next. At the Naples dock I watched the car until it disappeared around a corner. The sky was a clear blue, and a few high white clouds were drifting towards the south. I looked at my watch, finished my coffee and walked back to my hotel. I collected my bag, paid my bill and headed out to the airport.

PALERMO

As I sat in the lights of the afternoon airport, there was wool in my blood and clouds in my mind. My feet were swollen, and my eyes were wide. I sent Cora a text to tell her I was on my way to Palermo, waited ten minutes, and when I didn't get a reply I thumbed another that read: "Want me to bring you something back?" I looked at the words, but they didn't seem right. I deleted them and wrote "I'll buy you a present…" instead, waited a moment and let them go. I felt the electronic pulses that carried them, the perfect little flashes, and I thought about the speed of light. I wanted the speed of light in my life, and I wanted to feel its course.

The flight was nothing. I sat next to a fat woman who sat next to her fat son, and a drunk man caused a commotion when he tried to smoke in the toilet. I drank a miniature bottle of wine and crunched some nuts, and read the copy I'd written for the last edition of the *Tread Lightly Guide*.

Palermo is a contradiction. Correction. Palermo is a thousand contradictions. European or African? Relaxed or manic? Crime-free or watch-your-back? Loved or loathed? Italian or not? One thing is certain: scratch the surface, and you'll find whatever you want to find in this jewel of a city. Fancy some Byzantine architecture? You got it. A Renaissance Palazzo? No problem. Some Arab-Norman mosaics? Over there. A tropical garden? Just down the street. And if you need to give yourself a break from the treasure-hunting, step into one of the city's superb restaurants (and yes, they're all superb, no exceptions) and order the city's signature dish, pasta con le sarde. *The recipe varies, but expect onions, sardines, wild fennel, saffron, sultanas and pine nuts tossed over a mound of bucatini. Enjoy with a glass or two of Bianco d'Alcamo, and you have the makings of a perfect evening...*

I caught a taxi into town and lucked into a room in a hotel near Porta Carini. It had a balcony, and I could see the arch and columns of the ancient gate, and watch the bustle of the market, and listen to the neighbours sing, and smell cooking as it wafted up from a restaurant on the other side of the street. I took a shower, washed the grit off my skin and headed out.

The streets were filled with happy groups of people standing in little pools of light, but ten yards down the road the light was gone and the world was black. I took a side street that opened into a square with a broken fountain, headed down an alley that opened into a small square, turned left, left and right again and found myself in front of the Teatro Massimo. Twinkling lights wound around the columns of its portico, and people were climbing the steps to chat and mingle before taking their seats at the opera.

Cora and I once had an argument about opera. I claimed it was music written by egos, performed by egos and only to be enjoyed by egos. I then took my argument up a level by suggesting that opera was for people who couldn't enjoy real music, who didn't have the necessary attention span, who needed spectacle to help them understand. "It's a false art. In fact, it's not even art. It's wallpaper…" When she asked me if I'd finished and I said I had, she told me that she'd heard me come out with some bollocks before, but she thought that this time I had outbollocked myself. When I reeled off the names of a few opera lovers we knew, she said "OK. I'll give you that…" But when I tried to back up my thinking with some additional insights, she shook her head and said: "Just don't."

"Why not?"

"Because sometimes you just make me angry."

"And the rest of the time?"

"I'll say one thing."

"Go on then."

"*Soave sia il vento.*"

"Who?"

She said nothing.

I watched until the last people had disappeared into the theatre, and then I walked on. I passed bars and restaurants, but didn't stop until I came to a church. The doors were wide open, and it was crowded with singing families. Arms were swaying and smoke was rising through an orange light. I stepped inside, found a seat at the back and watched as children ran around and a priest read from the Bible. The words rang and a bell sounded, and as the echo of its chime clicked against the high roof, I thought about faith, miracles and prayer. I thought about faith and the Christian mysteries, but I got no answer from the questions I asked – and when, after half an hour, I stepped into the street and turned towards my hotel, my head felt empty and cold, ten below zero and falling.

LATE AND ZERO

I slept late, and when I woke I considered the wisdom of a hotel breakfast, women and their wet hair, old cheese and pale milk. I considered this plan for a couple of minutes, dismissed it, took a shower and padded out to the market to buy a pastry and coffee. When I got back to my room I sat on the balcony to eat and drink, and listened to the street and my head. It felt different, as if it was falling, failing even, or diving like the Paestum man. I could feel this falling, and although I knew all I had to do was reach out a hand and grab its wrist, I could not. I wanted to be good and free and easy, and I wanted to be happy, and I wanted what I knew I was losing, but what could I do?

I finished my breakfast and wandered out again, found myself at the quays, crossed three roads, almost got run over by a bus, took a table in a café with a view of the water, ordered coffee and sat to watch the ships and boats. A ferry arrived, gulls bothered the waves, and a man with a small dog walked by. I wrote some stuff in my notebook about coffee, closed my eyes and had a short daydream. It was about my Gran – my mother's mother – her collection of miniature tea sets, and how I used to visit her and have tea parties in her dark rooms. I opened my eyes, and my coffee was still hot. I drank it, dropped a handful of change on the table and headed back into town. I had work to do, so I found the place where buses left for Monreale, caught the first one I found and, as it climbed out of the city, I rested my arm on the edge of the open window and watched as people got on and off. Crowds of people were out, shopping for vegetables and fruit. An old woman climbed aboard with a bunch of flowers and a ginger cat in a string bag. I looked at the cat, and the cat looked at me, and when I looked at the old woman, she was looking at me too. It was a day of pairs.

When I reached Monreale, the bus dropped me by a café, and I walked through the town to the church. There was a sign on the door. It was closing within the hour, so I stepped inside and took a wander. Every surface of the place was covered in mosaic. A massive Christ with good hair watched me – the air twisted and glowed – clots of tired tourists stared and glazed. I stared and I glazed, and as I strolled a pain began to develop behind my eyes. It started like a like pinprick, but then it twisted and burrowed, and found a nerve. I needed fresh air, a place away from other people, and silence. I found a door that led to the cloisters, and here was a shaded spot where I could sit for a while and watch sparrows hunt for bugs. I counted eleven of the birds, and the counting eased the pain for a few minutes. I took out my notebook and wrote:

Monreale. The glittering Duomo of this, the finest Norman building in Sicily, reminds even the most casual visitor that although this was one of the most rapacious and avaricious dynasties that ever prowled the continent, it had the capacity – and foresight – to build some sublime cathedrals and adorn them with the most inspirational art. Packed with visitors in the season, in winter it echoes with a benign and easy silence...

I spent the rest of my time in Monreale in a state that swung between sadness and agitation. I wandered, watched a man making mosaic pictures and ate my lunch in a restaurant with small windows and cosy corners. The pain had returned – twitching inside my skull and whispering in my ears. It said: "You're lost, Matt. Why do you bother? Why don't you just admit it? You've got nothing, nothing to give anyone. Maybe you did once, but now – now you've got nothing. You're less than a loser. Even Cora thinks you're lost, and she knows you better than anyone..."

I was sitting at a table with a check tablecloth, and the waitress, a thin woman with black eyes, came over and asked me if I was all right. I told her I needed a cup of coffee, and she went to make one. An hour and a half later I was back in Palermo, lying on my bed with a jangling head and the idea that this was how I died.

EVENING

I dozed for an hour, and when I woke I felt weak but better, and ready to do something slowly. I swung my legs off the bed, put my feet on the floor, stood up and took a step towards the bathroom. The air appeared to shimmer around me, and I could smell cooking, but not in the usual way. This smell was sweet and intense, and seemed to have its own colour. I rubbed my eyes, reached the bathroom, turned on the shower and stepped in.

I closed my eyes, watched dots of light swarm in the dark and let the water do its work. I tipped my head back and let my mouth fill, and after ten minutes stepped out of the shower, wrapped myself in towels and checked my phone. I stared at the light and the icons, and tried to listen to its pulse. I heard nothing. I tossed it onto the bed and went to stand on the balcony.

Beyond the roofs and aerials, the horizon was a wound of orange and blue and scarlet, and the sounds of shouts and crying drifted up from the street. I sat down and thought about the dinner I hadn't eaten. Earlier, I'd seen two men cooking fish on a griddle set up under an awning. There were tables on the pavement, and the menu featured two dishes. Sardines with tomatoes or sardines with fennel.

I spent ten minutes wondering which I'd choose, and then I spent ten minutes thinking about words, and how sometimes I thought the things Cora and I said to each other were like paper lanterns strung across a crowded street, and how they swayed in the breeze and reflected against warm windows and doors that led to gardens. They could have been Japanese, but they weren't. Lovers could have looked up at them and smiled, and whispered things in each other's ears. They weren't sentimental words or words of promise, but they were meant. And boats could have appeared on narrow canals, oars dipping and falling, tassels swinging from embroidered canopies.

Then I thought about the future, and wondered if I had one. There are people who claim to see the future, but they fool themselves – they fool their friends, they lie. For in the same way that no one can return to the past, wipe away a mistake and live the life that should have been, no one can see what's coming. Some people use cards or entrails or the constellations because they're desperate to know what's around the corner. Other people choose to listen to the ravings of an old man or woman, someone who claims to hear the world in a cup. So I was ignorant. I was dumb. I didn't know anything. But how could I?

I sat on my Palermo balcony for about an hour, and as my thoughts chased themselves so they wore themselves out and my head began to clear. And with this head came the need to call Cora, so I sat back, imagined I was in the back of a taxi, thumbed her number, listened to the buzz and then we talked.

We started with pleasantries, the "where I was and what I was doing", the "where she was and what she'd been doing", and then the chat stopped at the lights. We needed to turn right. The indicators ticked and I waited for her to say something else. I listened. I could hear her breathing, and something else. It might have been the burble of her fridge, or it could have been the sound of London. I imagined her there, sitting at her kitchen table, two candles burning, a glass of wine casting its red light, a bowl of salad, a pile of unopened post – the smell of old oranges in a china bowl, a blue TV-screen light, a stolen beer mat I gave her last year.

I coughed.

She sniffed.

I stared up at the lights. They were still red. They weren't changing. I said: "Are you OK?"

"Yes."

"Sure?"

She slurped the wine. "I'm sitting down, but I'm on my feet."

"And what does that mean?"

"You know exactly what it means. You remember the song?"

"I do."

"It's one of my favourites."

"Don't I know it."

"Nothing beats it."

A car revved behind us, then stopped. "I think I know what our problem is," I said.

"I didn't know we had one."

"We miss each other when we're not together, but when we are together…"

"We don't like each other very much?"

"That's not what I was going to say."

"What were you going to say?"

"We spend too much time looking for each other's faults."

"Doesn't everyone?"

"Maybe," I said. "But that doesn't mean we have to."

"True. We could try and tolerate each other."

"Or we could…" I said, and then the lights changed – amber – green. I felt our car move forward.

"We could what, Matt?"

The car stalled.

"You want details?"

"Every single one."

"Let me think about that."

"You're a coward."

"I don't deny it."

I heard the chink of a bottle against the rim of a glass, the sound of pouring, and she said: "So…"

"So?"

"So what are you doing?"

"Now? Tomorrow?"

"Either. Both."

"I'm sitting on a balcony in Palermo. I was going to spend a few more days here, but I don't think I need them. I'm going back to Rome."

"Again? Why?"

"Why not?"

"I can't argue with that."

"It's a good place to work."

"And you've got plenty to do."

"I have. And you're going to tell me I could finish the job at home."

"Am I?"

"I hope so."

"You know that's not what we were talking about."

"I think…"

"You think what?"

"I think I should get an early night."

"That's not what you were going to say."

"It's not."

"So what were you going to say?"

I shook my head at nothing and the night. "I've got an early start."

"Matt?"

"Yes?"

I waited, and heard her take one of the deep, sighing breaths that used to irritate me so much. "Night," she said, and I held the phone to my ear for a moment and then she hung up. And as I sat at the table and watched the phone fade, I listened as Cora's voice echoed back at me, and I watched the years swirl their skirts and walk away.

WORK

Rome is a good place to work, but it's not the only place. As long as I have a table and a view, anywhere is a good place to work – a train, a tent, a shed, a bedroom – a blood-warm bath and a ripe vein. Music helps too, and tea, but these things are not essential.

So I worked, and my work was this: I had to take the material I'd gathered and bash it into shape. I could have carried on travelling for another month, but the brief had been to give the current guide a winter slant, a flavour. I didn't have to rewrite the entire guide. So I hadn't been to half the places I'd planned to visit, but who was to know? Tolstoy wasn't at Austerlitz, Beatrix Potter didn't go down a rabbit hole, Hemingway didn't tie a marlin to the side of a skiff and kill half a dozen sharks with a knife before falling asleep and drifting home on the gulf stream. I could imagine exactly what Lecce was like in February, and so I wrote exactly what Lecce was like in February.

The baroque masterpiece of Lecce is an architectural riot, a city of glorious palazzi and churches, most built from a honeyed sandstone. Take a stroll through the deserted streets on a winter's morning and you'll see the place in a

sharp, cold relief and give yourself an appetite for a warm-
ing lunch of the local delicacy: horse meatballs with wild
chicory and chickpeas. Follow this with a visit to the Basilica
di Santa Croce, an insane confection that appears to have
been designed by an acid head. Griffons, cherubs, dragons,
grotesques and other nightmares swarm over the façade,
and if you've the courage to risk your lunch, the interior has
the power to induce a reaction of the most violent kind…

I wrote this and wrote some more, then shut my laptop and
went for a walk – one foot in front of another. It was half-past
ten and the streets were quiet. The tourists had gone to their
beds, and the locals were watching football.

I like quiet streets, small bars, dry wine, shy cats, high
windows, the feel of squid, the taste of dust, steel, the idea
of bone and the memory of a time I stood naked in an empty
road at half-past three in the morning. It was drizzling and
I was drunk, and when I squinted, I could see a car driving
along a coast road miles away. The memory came from a long
time ago, when I was not happy.

And I like to watch people making things – pasta, a bowl,
a house, sweets. On one of the holidays my family took
when I was a kid, we visited a seaside town on the south
coast – Ramsgate, I think – and stood at a shop window to
watch women making sticks of rock. I don't remember how
they managed to get the letters into the rock, and although
I suppose I could find out how they do it, I won't. There are
things you want to do before you die and things you can't be

bothered to do before you die. That's death for you, and if you're lucky, you do a little of it every day, take a little victory and have a late dinner.

I headed towards Piazza della Rotonda and found a warm restaurant in a side street. I took my place at a table which would have been my favourite table if I'd been a regular, and ordered a carafe of Marino, a plate of *bucatini all'amatriciana* and a green salad. As I drank and listened to the chef sing as he worked, I took out my notebook.

If you have the time, or even if you don't, make a point of walking Rome by night, the later the better. It doesn't matter which quarter you explore, but it's difficult to beat the maze of little streets that fan away from the Pantheon. The ancient building might be the Temple of Every God, but that's not its true meaning, or its song. Look up as you walk, and the street lights will illuminate an edge to the city that the casual visitor is likely to miss: carved arches, scavenged reliefs, recessed statues, shuttered windows, crooked sills (either make your point or leave it).

My pasta arrived. It smelt of an orchard. The waiter offered pepper, and I let him grind. As I watched the grounds fall, I considered the fact that once pepper was worth more than its weight in gold. I turned my face, looked at the waiter and smiled. He nodded, lifted the mill and stepped away from the table. Maybe I would write something about the food later, but for now I allowed myself the luxury of living in the moment of eating. This is something my sister would have advised, her arms folded and her eyes half-closed as she contemplated the serenity of her life. I can't count the number of times she's told me that my problems are rooted in an inability to live in the moment. Of course everyone lives in the moment – it's just that sometimes the moment lasts years.

ONE HUNDRED WORDS
FOR TREE

Sometimes, when I sleep, I dream of people I used to know and see them as I wish they'd been. Sometimes they're glitter, breasts and smiles, and talking a language I don't understand even though I do in the dream. They swoon and sweep and leave their scent drifting in the air, and then they yawn and cuddle up for the night. And maybe they see the train in the night, and the pleasure of the dark. Or maybe they don't. I can't read the minds of people I used to know. They're best left in the past. They're best forgotten.

In the big room in the Roman hotel I had a large bed with a light duvet, and although the night was cold, I kept the window open so the sounds of the street drifted up as I waited for sleep. And the sounds of the street were attracted by my dreams and melted into them, so when I woke up at half-past six, I thought I'd been walking through a snowy market in a Norwegian town. I'd bought a garden ornament, a bag of nuts and some fruit, and by the time I got home, a little pyramid of snow had accumulated on top of my head, and icicles were growing from my ears. I lay and stared at the ceiling and waited for the feeling that I was cold to fade away. This took five minutes, and when I was ready, I got up, showered and went down for breakfast. A woman was sitting in the corner, drinking coffee and eating a pastry. Her hair was damp and she was wearing a white blouse. I smiled when she wished me a good morning, poured a cup of coffee, spooned fruit into a bowl, picked a newspaper off a table, read the headline, decided I didn't need to know about the Prime Minister's holiday preferences and went to sit at a table by the door.

I was eating a piece of grapefruit when a text arrived. Cora. "Not feeling so good. Working from home. Talk if you want."

Cora hardly ever took a day off, so when I'd finished my breakfast and was back in my room, I called her. "You OK?"

"Yeah. It's just a cold."

"But you never get colds."

"Well, I have now."

"I'm sorry," I said, but I knew she didn't have a cold.

"It's not your fault."

I was going to tell her that I knew it wasn't my fault, and my saying sorry was not an apology, but I told her about my dream instead, and when I'd explained that sometimes I think dreams are simply your mind taking a dump, she said: "You've told me that before."

"And what did you say?"

"I don't remember."

She sniffed, but it wasn't a real sniff.

"OK. Anyway…"

"Anyway what?"

"While I was having my breakfast, I was thinking about snow and that thing about Sámi people having a hundred words for the stuff."

"What's so amazing about it?"

"I guess when a Sámi looks at a tree, all they see is a tree. Whereas we have a hundred words for tree – more than a hundred, in fact: oak, ash, sycamore, holly, beech…"

"Those are different types of tree, not different words for tree."

"Exactly. And if you were a Sámi and all you'd ever seen was a pine tree, you wouldn't be arguing."

She gave me another silence and sniffed again. "Sometimes, Matt…"

"Sometimes what?"

"Sometimes you make me want to scream."

"But you get my point, don't you?"

"Right now I'm struggling to get any point to anything." I heard a rustling and then she blew her nose. "Have you checked your email?"

"Not yet."

"You should have one from head office – subject line 'Rebranding'. Read it."

"All right. And I was going to say… I've got a couple of things to do here, and then I'm coming home."

"Already?"

"Yes."

"Why?"

"Because… Because I…" and then I felt something crack in the wires between us.

"OK."

"Are you going to ask me what those things are?"

"Not really. But it sounds like you want to tell me."

I did, but I wasn't going to. "All I'm going to tell you is to go to bed with some honey and lemon. Get better."

GOLD

I did as I was told and tried to check my emails, but the broadband was down or slow or both, so I grabbed my coat, headed out and strolled to the Piazza di Spagna. The day was bright and blue and cold. Here and there, piles of slush hid in corners.

I reached the square. I suppose I knew what I was doing, but supposing is one thing, doing it another. I went to the antique shop where I'd seen the pretty cat. The window display had been changed: the painting of Christ calming the waters had been replaced by a pastoral scene, and an ornate pair of chairs had taken the place of the papier-mâché globes.

I rang the shop's doorbell, listened to it echo in the distance and watched a pigeon standing on a window sill. A key turned, and Signor Buonarroti opened the door. He was slipping his coat off his shoulders. He squinted at me and then smiled. "Signor Baxter?"

"Signor Buonarroti."

He offered me his hand. We shook, and he stepped to one side and beckoned me inside, closed the door and said: "It's a pleasure to see you again".

"I'm afraid I've been away longer than a week, but I thought I'd come back and see…"

He held up his hand. "Of course. I thought about you last week, and I wondered if you'd visit again. I did wait a couple more days, but then I'm afraid I had to put the piece back on show."

"That's a shame."

"But no one has wanted to see it…" He smiled and patted my shoulder. "So, if you wish?"

"Thank you," I said, and I followed him down the corridor, past the galleries of furniture and watercolours, the antiquities and statuary. The smell of polish and cigars was still strong and sweet, and as the clocks ticked and the soft atmosphere drifted, I listened to my shoes on the floor and the rustle of my coat. I stopped for a moment at a case I hadn't noticed before. It contained a collection of small, bright coins, arranged in concentric circles and lit by a dust of light. Each coin featured a simple design: there were back-to-back crescent moons, sheaves of corns, wheels and prancing horses – lots of prancing horses.

"From your country, Signor Baxter. They're Celtic staters. Pure gold."

"They're beautiful," I said, and we carried on walking to the room of cabinets. He went to a bureau, found a bunch of keys and jangled them in his hand. "The keys to paradise," he said, and I smiled.

I stood behind him as he unlocked the glass and took the brooch out and handed it me. I'd been right. It wasn't the most beautiful object in the world, but it was close. The tiny green eyes, the almost scowl on the cat's face, the almost flawless pearl, the delicate curl in the tail, the satisfying heft. Maybe I wasn't so hopeless at buying presents.

"I think," said Signor Buonarroti, "that even the most beautiful of women would become, how can I say, more gorgeous with this on…"

"I think you're right," I said. "1,200 Euro?"

"It is."

"Then I'll take it."

"You're a wise man, Signor Baxter."

"In some things, Signor Buonarroti. Only some things."

"Ah…" he said. He smiled and patted my shoulder, then took the brooch from me and stepped to the bureau, opened a drawer and took out a small red box. "Here," he said. "A safe home for a very special cat."

I gave him my bank card to pay, and once the transaction was completed, he opened the box, clipped the brooch inside, tapped its head, closed the lid and said: "I have a bag, if you wish?"

"It's fine like this," I said – and it was. He smiled and handed the box to me. I slipped it into my pocket, and he walked me down the corridor to the front door. He opened it and said: "You know, you are very welcome to come back any time."

"Thank you."

"No," he said. "That is not for you to say. Let other people say that today."

GIBBERISH

I sat at a window table in a small bar, ordered a coffee, took the brooch out of its box and turned it over in my hand. Away from Signor Buonarroti's gallery, it wasn't close to being one of the most beautiful objects in the world. In truth, in a certain light, it was a piece of kitsch and, in another light, a crude lump of Victorian sentimentality. But sentimentality is underrated, and so is kitsch, and every life benefits from a light dusting of the stuff. Condiments, if you will, or barrettes. And Cora often wore a barrette for no other reason than it looked pretty – and why should she have to have any other reason? People love to have reasons. But is there any lovelier sound than the words "no reason at all"? Of course there is. There's the sound of cheese hitting marble, the pounding of rain on a tin roof, the squeak of a comfy mouse or the squeal of a baby when it sees its breakfast – a tune drifting from a high balcony. I put the brooch back in its box, drank my coffee and took out my phone and checked my messages. One from Cora said "You read the email yet?" I thumbed "Just about to", logged on and opened my inbox. I scrolled through to one with the subject "CEO Visit Conclusions – Rebranding" and read.

The CEO had written a report based on the visit he'd made to the London office the day after I'd arrived in Italy, and a decision had been made: Tread Lightly was going to be rebranded – and, more than that, the company was being "rationalized". The idea of treading lightly was going to be pushed to the max, and my trip to Italy was going to be the last of its kind. From now on, going forward, thinking future-wise, the focus was going to be exclusively on sustainable, environmentally friendly tourism. We were going to live our ethos, and this meant we would suggest ways of travelling that didn't require flying: we'd encourage people to get involved with the local communities they visited, and we'd promote efforts to conserve and enhance the ecosystems they visited.

"Ah…" I said to my coffee, and I picked up the cup and sipped. I read the email again, thought about the idea of living an ethos and then, supported by my own honesty and unwilling to take any more nonsense from either myself or the world, I called Cora.

There were no pleasantries this time, just: "So, you read it?"

"Yeah." I said.

"And?"

"Apart from the gibberish, what exactly is environmentally friendly tourism? Is it as comparatively unique as I think it is?"

"What?"

"Or is he taking the idea that there's truth in advertising to its oxymoronic conclusion?"

"You're going to have to explain yourself, Matt. I think my cold has turned my head to mush."

"OK. How can you possibly have sustainable tourism? Even if you don't fly, even if you only ever take ferries or trains or ride a bike, the world is screwed another degree. The only way to really tread lightly is either to stay at home or travel by foot. And even then, once you arrive, all you're really doing is putting an intolerable strain on your hosts. So you might be making a contribution to the local economy, but what sort of contribution are your making to the local ecosystem? It's like those cans of 'sustainably fished tuna' that inform the happy shopper that it's 'dolphin-friendly'. It's not very friendly to the tuna…"

"Sorry, Matt. I didn't realize. You're back."

"What do you mean?"

"Back to your old cynical self." She coughed. "Not that it ever really went away." She didn't sound well. "But whatever. You know, I sort of missed it."

"No, Cora. I'm not being cynical, sarcastic, sceptical or any of the other things you want me to be. I'm just stating the obvious – maybe the truth. The first time I went to Bangkok, the airport was a strip of tarmac and a corrugated shed in a paddy field. Now look at it…"

"The truth?"

"Yes."

She laughed.

"It's like something I was reading the other day…"

"Oh God…"

"…about a group of environmentalists who sailed to Greenland. They wanted to learn about climate change and glacial melting and the decimation of arctic wildlife, and there was a picture of them wearing plastic clothes, standing on front of their boat, smoke belching from the funnel, about to get into a polyurethane speedboat to go and get a closer look at some icebergs. And two of them were carrying rifles, in case a polar bear got too close…"

"Hello?"

"Though I should say not all of them were professional environmentalists. One of them was a composer, and he'd been commissioned to write an opera about the effects of global warming on glaciers, and another was a novelist, and she…"

"Matt!" She shouted now. "I don't think you've read the right email. The one about rebranding was sent yesterday."

"Was it?"

"Yes."

"The one you were meant to read was sent this morning. Subject: 'CEO, further conclusions'. Read it and phone me back," she said, and she hung up.

I suppose I deserved it, but I was trying to make a point. Obviously. But neither of us are patient, and as I sat back and finished my coffee, and scrolled through my emails to the one I'd been meant to read, I mused on the fact that, in a world of deceit, maybe the people who see the most truth are the ones who lie most deeply.

"CEO, further conclusions" was short and, although more to the point than the other, was still ambiguous. But this time the ambiguity was easy to read, and quick and sharp. The key concept was "virtual inter-participation": in the future, all Tread Lightly's written collateral would be produced by its customers – blogs, emails, SM posts, reviews – all would be drawn together and reassembled in an online notebook. With this in mind, "rationalization" was being applied to the London office, which was being closed. Twenty-seven people were being "let go". I was one of them, Cora was another.

I let this information drop and sink. Being sacked over the phone for telling your boss you'd seen her arse in a 2,000-year-old fresco was one thing – being rationalized so your job could be done for free by illiterates was something else completely. I picked up my phone, looked at the screen and hit redial. But before it rang, I saw someone I recognized. She stopped outside the bar, checked her watch, pushed the door and stepped inside. I hung up, checked the corners of my mouth for crumbs and stood up.

THE SHADOWS

Coincidence is life when it's bored. One minute you're doing what you've always done – you're getting up in the morning, you're having breakfast, eating toast and drinking tea while you tell yourself that what you do is important and vital and serious – you leave the house and stroll to the station and stand on a platform for ten minutes, ride the Tube for half an hour, walk through the streets to your office, sit at a desk, stare at a screen, say hello to your colleagues as they drift in, and you wonder what it's like for people who don't have to do this every day, people who are free, even though you know they're really not free. No one's free, you think, and you start to get caught in a swirl of contradiction and trouble before you've strolled to your first meeting, which is about a series of mini city guides that are going to be given away free with airline tickets. They're going to be called "Taster Tips". And as you sit and listen to someone talk about Berlin, you look at the other people in the meeting and speculate. The designer with a beard like the bloke from that film about someone building a house in Spain – or was it Portugal? – does he really believe this project is ground-breaking, or has he pushed his creative walrus so far up the beach that it thinks it's a sun lounger? And the intern with short hair and her grandma's brooch pinned in her hair – is she really prepared to work past close of play to get the index pages sorted? And the account handler who's seen *Les Misérables* every week for two years – is she really going to give up eating chocolate? And the guy from production – is he really going to stab me in the throat with a scalpel if I go near his cutting mat again, or is that an empty threat? And then it's lunch, so the meeting folds and you go to a sandwich shop on the other side of the street, because if you go to the café on the second floor you'll have to sit next to the art director, who ducked out of the meeting and spent the morning cruising YouTube for ideas. And as you sit in the sandwich shop and watch the rain, everyone who passes by looks free, even the man who sweeps the streets.

And the afternoon rolls on. You sit at your desk and write something about Prague, and you turn down an offer to go for a drink after work, and you change your mind about going to the cinema on Wednesday, and you watch the Head of Brand Strategy appear from the lift and saunter to the Chief Editor's office. You watch them wave their arms at each other, and voices are raised, and you get up and walk to the far end of the floor to the coffee machine, and you make a cup of tea and stare at the inside of the fridge and laugh because you heard someone say: "The creatives are going bowling on Friday."

So, one minute you're doing what you've always done, and then you're doing it again. You're getting up in the morning, you're having breakfast, eating toast while you tell yourself that what you do is important and vital and serious. You leave the house and stroll to the station and stand on a platform for ten minutes, and for no particular reason you start to think about your cousin. He used to live in London, but moved to Amsterdam, bought an antiquarian bookshop and a flat with a view of a peaceful canal, and now he sits in his shop all day and reads, and occasionally sells a rare and expensive book to a millionaire. And as you ride the train and walk through the streets to your office, you think "Lucky bastard…" – and as you stare at your screen and think about what you're going to say in the first meeting of the day, the phone rings. You're not going to answer it, but something tells you to. The something was wise and knew something you didn't. Because it's your cousin calling from Amsterdam, and he gets straight to the point. He always did. He's a dynamic chap with a friendly, approachable manner, and he asks if you remember what you'd said last year about working in his shop, and when you say that you do, he says he's opening a new shop in Utrecht, and would you be interested in working as the manager of the shop in Amsterdam? He knows you speak a few languages, and he knows you love books. You could start whenever you want, but sometime next month would be good. Coincidence or just life?

So I was sitting in a corner of a Roman café, protected by shadows and four days' stubble. I'd ordered a second cup of coffee. My head was clear, and I was doing what I was meant to be doing. But my head and the shadows and stubble didn't protect me from a sudden rush of blood or adrenaline or whatever it is you get when coincidence meets excitement and kicks its teeth. My heart started beating faster: I felt a creeping in my legs and tingling in my fingers.

This latest coincidence and the face from the past belonged to Emily Paget, and it told an old story, a story that's been and gone a million times. We met at university, and for a couple of years were inseparable. The details are prosaic – I was studying English, she was studying History; the city was Canterbury and the flat we shared for the last two terms was in a house on Suffolk Road – but at the time we believed we were far from prosaic, and our love was complete. We made plans for the future. We'd move to London – I'd get a job at the British Museum, she'd get a job at the British Library. We'd live on a boat on Regent's Canal. Some weekends we'd take the boat out, some weekends we'd take the train to the coast, some weekends we'd just stay in bed and eat croissants. Ducks would quack, the water would lap – we'd be safe in our cradle.

But this was the story never told – the one that was more obvious. We left university, we couldn't get work, we returned to our family homes, we phoned each other every evening, we told each other we had to be patient. One day, she said she'd been offered a job at Birmingham Central Library. The following week I was offered a job in Clerkenwell as a junior writer for a company that published trade magazines.

For six months, flushed with money and plans and ambition, we met at weekends, sometimes in London, sometimes in Birmingham, a few times at a hotel in Cambridge. We'd walk and talk and walk some more, but when autumn came, we knew. Our silences were freighted with something unsaid, something neither of us could articulate. So when one day, as we sat in a pub in Canonbury and she said she'd met someone called George, I already knew. I think I even knew his name. It felt familiar. I nodded, and when she said "Hey, we can still be friends, can't we?" I said "Of course" – but of course we couldn't. You can't crash a car and expect to make a bicycle from the bits. You just walk away and know that life goes on. You string yourself along with as many clichés as you can and then, years later, you double-take when you see her walking into a small Roman café. So we might have become crooked, fighting eclipses, but we still recognized our discs. I looked at her and she looked at me – we both looked away and a moment later looked back at each other. I opened my mouth, and she said: "Matt?"

"Emily?"

"My God. It is you…"

"What are you doing here?"

I pointed to the table. "Having a cup of coffee."

"Amazing…"

"I know…"

"Can I?" She pointed to the table.

"Of course."

She sat down – I sat down and looked at her face. It hadn't changed much – maybe a line had appeared here and another there, and her hair was shorter, but she was still beautiful Emily. I said: "So…"

"So…"

"And what are you doing here?"

"We're just having a few days…"

"We?"

"Chris and I."

"Chris? I thought it was George."

"George? No." She lifted her finger and showed me the rings on her finger.

"You're married?"

"Oh yes. Ten years."

"Wow."

"I know."

The waiter came over, and when I suggested a glass of wine, she said: "Why not?"

"How long's it been?" I said.

"Since when?"

"Since, you know, we..."

She shrugged. "Twenty years?"

"At least."

"But you haven't changed."

She laughed and touched her hair. "A few grey ones in there, but thank you..."

"It's true. Kids?"

She shook her head. "No."

"And you're still in Birmingham?"

"No. Moved years back. Chris got a job in Cheltenham. I can't tell you what he does, but then he can't tell me what he does." She tapped the side of her nose.

"And you?"

"Still a librarian."

"A happy librarian?"

She shrugged. "Define your terms."

I laughed. She used to say that to me, and my laugh reminded her – and as she dropped her eyes, the years seemed to drop away, and we were students again, and wine was cheap and we smoked cigarettes, and we had time for anyone.

"What's funny?" she said.

"I was just thinking…"

"What?"

I shrugged. "So many years, Emily, but it doesn't feel like it."

She smiled. "And you?"

"And me what?"

"What are you doing?"

"Still in London, though I moved south of the river. Writing for Tread Lightly."

"The travel books?"

"Yes."

"That must be your dream job."

"Less of a dream now. I've just been made redundant."

"I'm sorry."

I shrugged. "I only just heard, but you know what?"

"What?'

"I'm not sure I care. I was beginning to lose the plot. It's probably the best thing that could've happened. I can get a job washing dishes and do some proper writing…"

She laughed. "That's what you were going to do twenty years ago. Except, then you were going to sell freshly squeezed orange juice from a cart on a street corner…"

I remembered that. That was a plan. "Dream big, Emily. Dream big."

Our wine arrived. We chinked glasses, and I wondered.

"I did write a couple of novels, but that was the easy bit. Try getting one published."

"You tried?"

"Oh yeah. I got an agent and everything. I've still got him, though I never get a Christmas card."

"And how's…" – she took a gulp of wine – "your love life?"

Now I laughed.

"That funny?"

"It's complicated."

"Wasn't it always?"

"I suppose it was."

"Tell me."

"She's my boss. Was my boss. She's been made redundant too. We split up a few months back, but it never really ended."

"In your mind or hers?"

"Now that's a good question." I drank. "But you were always good with questions."

"Wasn't I?"

"You were," I said, and so it went, the two of us catching up, clawing back the years into a bundle of conversational hesitation, both of us seeing the gap that had appeared between us, but not caring, not really. For there was no recrimination, no sadness or blame, nothing to heal or mend. Just a pleasant hour of chat, and the things most profound were the things left unsaid. This – I thought – was how it should always be, how friends and lovers and family should be. Sweeping sadness and cliché into its pit and smiling at the past, for what is the past if not but a rage of notes that become sweet? And what is sweetness if not its own bitter echo? So when I said "Remember that day in Cambridge?" and she said "The one with the punt?" and I said "Yes" and she said "Did you ever find your shoe?" I knew we'd made a connection that went beyond the banality of love and found its power in the ease of a river.

"I never found my shoe," I said, "but I didn't want to. What was the point? It was summer. You don't need shoes in the summer."

"Our summer."

"We had a few."

"We had one," she said, and as she said the words she looked at me with the eyes I remembered, and for a moment I felt myself flailing. I think she did too, for now there was a crackle in the air between us. I said "Emily..." and she let her eyes drop and reached across the table for my hand, took it in hers and squeezed. The surprise of her touch shocked me, and she said "One long summer..." – and as the words flapped and tried to take off, the door opened and a man I knew was Chris stepped into the café. Emily snatched her hand away, and her eyes dropped, and he saw her and came to where we were sitting and looked at his wife with a narrowed eye and a newspaper under his arm. She stood up, and I stood up, and she said: "Chris – this is Matt. Matt – Chris..."

"Hi," I said, and we shook hands. He looked confused and puzzled, and lost in Rome. I broke the spell by taking a step backwards and looking at my watch. I wasn't interested in the time, but pretended I was. "Great to meet you," I said to him, and then I turned to Emily. "And to see you again."

"And lovely to see you too."

And so I leant towards her and she held out her hand. I took it and felt something stiff in my hand, and when I looked into her eyes she pleaded. Then the pleading dropped, and like the thief I palmed her card, and she said something about not leaving it so long next time, and I laughed like an old friend, and Chris narrowed his eyes – and I picked up my bag and left the café.

People say "Don't look back", but I ignore people and their foolish advice. I looked back and saw Chris waving his arms and Emily shrugging, and Chris raising his hand and Emily flinching, and Chris turning and Emily not, and people at the other tables staring and wondering. I'd sensed the edge two minutes before, and now I watched it splay, but as I walked through the streets and let the early afternoon light wash over me, I was calm and relaxed, and quiet. And something she'd said reminded me. The meeting with her had flicked a switch, and something had cleared. And as I strolled towards the beautiful streets and dropped her card in a bin, it was as though I'd cleared ivy from a low door in a wall, moved away from the dulling of a shadow I knew was there but couldn't see and stepped into a sunlit garden. There were fountains playing and gravel paths – and, in the distance, the promise of bells ringing over a spring.

CALLING

I sat on a low wall in a quiet street and called Cora. She answered on the second ring with "You took your time".

"I was thinking."

"You read it?"

"Yes."

"And?"

"I was on the way out, Cora. You know that. I'll find something else. People need copy."

"Sure…" She sniffed.

"But I was thinking about you."

I heard rustling and then she blew her nose.

"What are you going to do?" I said.

"I don't know. It's a shock, Matt. I knew something was coming, but not this. I didn't think I'd feel like this, but I'm bowled over." She sighed. "They just closed the entire office…"

"I know…"

She took a deep, watery breath. "The bastards. I've got half a mind to jack the whole thing in."

"I know the feeling."

"Do you?"

"Yes," I said, and I raised my voice. "I know the feeling *exactly*, Cora."

She felt the shock of that.

"I'm sorry," I said.

"Forget it."

"I didn't mean to shout. Forgive me?"

"I'm tired, Matt. So tired. Sometimes I think…"

"What?"

"We orbit."

"What did you say?"

"We orbit – but we never, I don't know… we never touch."

Silence.

"Cora?"

Nothing.

I shook my phone.

"Hello?"

Nothing.

"Cora?"

Silence.

"Cora?"

The last silence.

"Hello?"

The last hello.

I waited a moment, but then she wailed, and I heard the sound of the kicking of a chair, the smashing of something against a wall, another wail and the spin of coins – the rage of beauty against brick. And then my phone started to buzz, and then it was dead – and I was left holding the dead and useless thing, the electric nipple that keeps us connected but so apart and so failed.

THE MYTH OF INSPIRATION

I tried to call her back – once, twice and then a third time – but each ring went to voicemail. So I thumbed a text – "Call me when you can" – grabbed my coat and walked the streets around Piazza Navona for an hour. As the evening fell, I found myself outside a bar. You know the form: it was a Roman thing, a hint of casual, a pair of cats, some touch of beauty and a scale of notes drifting from somewhere you think you remember. I pushed the door open, and the warmth rolled out and spilt over the cobbles. I stepped inside, and the door swung behind me. A waiter came from the back and smiled and offered me a seat at a corner table.

I ordered a beer, sat back and looked around. A couple were sitting at a window table, smiling and laughing. The man said something, leant towards the woman, kissed her neck and pointed at her wineglass. She smiled and nodded. She was a beautiful woman with long brown hair. When the light caught it, reddish highlights shimmered against the brown. She had a pianist's hands and wore rings on her fingers, and a little bracelet around her right wrist. He looked happy and comfortable. They looked like they'd spent the last five days in bed, making love, reading books, listening to birdsong and eating cheese. She had a beautiful, open face, and when it caught a shadow it changed slightly as if it could be a hundred different faces but this was the one it was now.

The waiter brought my beer and a bowl of olives, and as I drank I thought about faces, feathers and Bakelite, and I thought about windows. I had no idea how glass was made, radios worked or eggs were laid, or why the sky was blue, the sea was salt or birds sang, but now I was going to find out. I was going to learn and I was going to buy a microscope. So maybe I still had some sort of control disorder or had a mis-alignment in my neuro meta-triggers, but I was getting too old to care. And even though I was still, I was moving, and as I drank and nibbled, I considered this: we all rob. We rob from the Cambodian woman who makes our shirts, and we rob the child who picks the bananas we slice over our muesli. We rob the cabbie of his health, animals of their lives and the sea of its blue. There's no fine line, no difference and no peculiarity. Like a friend I used to have who travelled to the Maldives and spent three months visiting its islands because she wanted to understand the effects of climate change on the population of a drowning country, we're all strolling towards the edge so beautifully, all so eager and so handsome, our fingers in our ears and our eyes covered with our own dirty hands. What more can you do but admire our blindness?

I admired my bag. It was leather and old, and had been with me to around thirty countries. It was scuffed, and its handles were frayed, and it had a good zip. I thought about zips. They were simple, but complicated and precise. If they weren't carefully engineered, they were useless, and if they were useless, their engineering was pointless. This is how my thoughts went, and I allowed them to do whatever they wanted. I think they helped me. My thoughts have taken me to more places than my feet have ever done. I was never cruel or heartless, but I could be forgetful, and I was.

There's a myth about inspiration – the myth of an internal stimulus provoked by something external. A scent, the atmosphere in a particular room, the view from a cliff, the sound of a particular chord, the presence of other people, the sense of a lover – the leaving somewhere familiar and arriving somewhere new, the substitution of grey for green, a wall for a window.

I would say inspiration is an excuse: I don't have it, you can't find it, she's lost it, he never had it. Someone once said to me: "Just write the thing down, finish it, and when you've got to the end, and only then, start editing. You're an instinctive writer, Matt, and sometimes you're almost a good one." I wouldn't suggest that you should apply another's rules to your own work, but when advice is that simple, it's worth noting. And as Cora said, "You might be a hack, but that doesn't mean you're a fraud. Not necessarily, anyway." Sometimes differences expose such plain simplicities.

Cora and I started as colleagues, and although we became lovers, there was always resistance in our relationship. Times were good, times were bad, money slipped through our fingers – we sniped and pretended we knew where we were going. We lived like the weather, and when she talked, people stopped to listen, and when she walked, they took a step back. If she had been a noble gas, she would have been neon. She often

looked like she was about to take something back to a shop – a
pair of trousers that did not fit, a lampshade she didn't like
as much as she thought she did. If I had been a noble gas, I'd
have been argon, and when I told her this, she laughed and
said: "That makes sense. You are inactive." I once told her
that I thought I would have made a good ferryman.

"A ferryman?" she said.

"Yes."

"Why?"

"Because I like taking people from one place to another."

"Then be a bus driver," she said.

"I want to work on water," I said.

"OK," she said. "Then be a ferryman."

"Or a fisherman…"

"A ferryman, a fisherman… whatever, Matt. Choice isn't
a luxury."

Choice isn't a luxury.

Remember this.

I ordered another beer, and as I drank I took out my phone
and sent Cora a line. "OK?" I thumbed, and the waiter brought
some more olives.

"No…"

"I'm home the day after tomorrow."

"So?"

"Fancy a drink?"

"That depends."

"On?"

"If you're there."

"And if I am?"

"You'd better be."

"Promises, promises."

The couple at the window table exchanged another kiss. She said something, and he laughed. She reached up and stroked the side of his head and caught my eye. I smiled at her, she smiled back, and I wondered if Cora and I could become like these people, never doubting each other or feeling we had to say something. And I wondered – do people talk because they're scared that if they stop talking they'll start thinking? I read somewhere that they do. But whatever, I thought. Cora and I have some history, and maybe that's all anyone can hope for. That and owning the tinkling promise of thoughts, a collection of photographs and a decent leather bag.

THE SOUTH IN SPRING

I have no idea if the winterized copy I wrote for Tread Lightly was published, but I don't care, for in the time between leaving Italy and returning to England and doing what I had to do and returning to Italy, and then going back to England one last time, something Daniel and I had talked about in Rome coalesced, focused and became a truth to me, and it was this: writing is a pollution. Like an island of plastic in the ocean, it drifts and shifts, changes shape, chokes waves and kills the living.

The man said: "You can't *want* to write, you *have* to write…" – and although these words took the cash and spent it in your favourite bar, no one took any notice, because they were too busy writing their own stuff – blogs – poems – memoirs – posts – novels – comments – journals – films – reviews – songs – raps – plays – tweets. The word is mightier than the sword? You bring your Graf von Faber-Castell, I'll bring my Masamune, and we'll prove Ahikar wrong. And when we're done, let me count the cuts. Here. I have none and you are dead. I have killed, but am no murderer. Stupidity is proved by the clever without their knowledge. I haven't spoken since dawn because I've been working, and my day started early.

When Cora and I were made redundant and decided to make a fresh life, we made a deal – we'd leave the things we'd done behind us and paint a new door. So we spent a few days talking about the past, reminding ourselves of the mistakes we'd made and the things we'd done right, and forgiving each other for wrongs.

She told me Picasso believed art was a lie that makes us realize truth, and I told her Lennon had been wrong when he said "all you need is love". Lennon imagined it was that easy, but it's the other way round – love needs you, and it demands and expects. You work for love, at love, over love. You fight for it, and there are no short cuts. There's no walking in the rain, no running your fingers through anything, no dancing in moonlight. Romance is water, and romance is nonsense. And if you want to know how I know, read the copy I spent half a lifetime writing. I know about drawing melodies on the face of rage.

So on the last day of April, I took the notebooks I'd filled with ideas, the manuscripts of novels completed and half-finished, the doggerel I'd passed off as poetry, the stories for kids and the rest, stuffed them in a bag and caught a train to the coast. I found a sheltered spot beneath the cliffs between Ramsgate and Broadstairs, made a neat pyre of the stuff and, while I drank a bottle of Giuseppe Quintarelli's Amarone della Valpolicella Classico, I watched the pages burn. Thirty-two years of ideas, imagination, hope, nonsense, fancy and ambition flamed and smoked, and as the paper carbonized and the words turned to their negative, they were taken by the breeze and lifted into the sky and carried east, across the water and higher until the horizon was smudged with their last gasp. One pollution cleared to be replaced by another. And then, nothing.

My father was ill for a couple of years before he died, and spent the last six months of his life muttering things like "Please let me go..." and "Why can't I die?" – and as the last blackened pages twirled and failed, I felt an echo of the emotions I'd felt as I watched the old man fade – sorry to see him go, but glad his pain was over. For these pages, these words and ideas and noise had been my pain, and their destruction a relief. Now I could say that I had no ambition, and with ambition gone I was free. And as a free man, I walked along the sea wall to Broadstairs and a hotel five doors down from my mother's flat.

I spent a few days with my mother, took her out for dinner and walks along the beach, and joined her and Mrs Babinski at a performance of Mendelssohn's *Elijah* at the parish church. When the terrors were done and the Lord God had calmed down and answered the prophet's prayers, and the quartet sang "Oh come everyone that thirsteth", the music lifted me like a mote, and when the organ began to rumble in the final chorus, I felt my skin prickle. Later, as we sat in her sitting room and shared a bottle of something sweet, I told her I was moving, and she said "That's nice dear" – and when I told her I was going to do something different with my life, she said: "Your father always said he was going to do something different with his life, but he never did. Hastened his end, I think." And she reached out, took my hand and said: "Change is the spur that never killed the horse."

"Is it? I said.

"Yes," she said, and she reached into her purse and gave me a pound coin. I was going to remind her that I was a forty-nine-year-old man and didn't need pocket money, but the giving was such a pleasure to her, so I thanked her, kissed her cheek and told her that once I was settled she was to visit.

"I don't think it's changed much from when you were there."

"And when was that?"

"1965, I think."

Cora and I walked away because we could. We knew we were lucky, and know we are. She sold her flat and I sold mine, and we wrote letters to the people we could leave, and the people we loved. We did the things we were meant to do, said the words we were born to say, bought a pair of tickets and flew.

We bought an apartment in Salerno. It's small and has a terrace, and if you duck through the bedroom window and climb nine steps, you'll find two chairs and a table, and a view of the harbour and the bay. We bought an apartment and we bought an espresso trike from Piero, the brother of the man who owns the shop on the corner of the street. Piero knows people, and as long as we leave him an envelope every other Friday, we're good.

Our lives are reduced, and although we have a radio, we don't listen to it in the evening. Our lives are reduced, and although we rescued books from our previous lives, we don't bother with them. Their pages keep the words quiet, and we agree, and this is our day.

Every morning, I go to the garages behind our apartment, fire up the trike, buzz it through a gate and down the road. It rattles and creaks, but it won't break down, and I park it on a pitch on the corner. I've been doing this for six months, and I have regulars. The family who keep a café by the station had a few words with me, but when I told them about Piero the words stopped. This is a quiet town.

I sell coffee and pastries, and fruit. I do good in the world, give pleasure, make friends and, some time before noon, when people are thinking about their lunch, I fire up the trike again and ride it back to the garage.

Sometimes Cora's home and sometimes she's not, and sometimes she leaves me a note to tell me she's gone for a walk and we'll meet in a bar.

We meet in a bar by the cathedral and take a table by the window. Sometimes she wears the brooch I bought in Rome and sometimes she leaves it on a table in our apartment and wears a flower. She's not a sentimental woman, and since she left London she's let her hair grow. These days she eats more cheese and drinks more wine. I drink more wine too, but we're functional.

She has her own plans, but they're her own business. If you want to know what they are, ask her. And if you want to know how you're supposed to do that, ask yourself how the sun will dip this evening, or how it will rise from the box of your life, or from wherever you keep it. For now, in this year and place, we are as the wise thrush who sings each song twice – and as the foxes cry over the bins and the waves fish the bay beyond our terrace, the pareidolia of a cat follows the folds in the shadows of our blinds.